Wanted:
ONE GROOM

Pat Ballard

Pearlsong Press
Nashville, TN

Pearlsong Press
P.O. Box 58065
Nashville, TN, 37205
www.pearlsong.com

ISBN: 0-9713247-0-0
Library of Congress Control Number: 2004104466

This book contains the text of the 2000 softcover edition
published by Writers Club Press, an imprint of iUniverse.com, with
minor revisions.

Other books by Pat Ballard available from Pearlsong Press:

Dangerous Curves Ahead
A Worthy Heir
His Brother's Child
Nobody's Perfect

*To my husband, Joe, and my son, Eric,
just because I love them.*

Chapter 1

"Hanna, you know what your grandfather's will stipulated." Hanna sensed the barely concealed agitation in her mother's voice.

"But, just in case you've forgotten, let me refresh your memory," chimed in Hanna's brother, Will, two years her senior. "You have to be married, in order to receive the money that the old codger left you. And if you aren't married by the time you're thirty years old, everything goes to charity." Will didn't try to conceal the contempt he felt for his grandfather, not only for leaving him totally out of the will except for a substantial monthly allowance, which he blew on a monthly basis, but for leaving the conditions as such that they might all wind up on the streets with nowhere to live.

"Everything, Hanna," interjected her mother. "That means this house, all the land that goes with the estate, all the furniture in the house, and all the money in the bank, including our allowances. Are you going to let that happen to us? To your brother and me, and to yourself?" Desperation was apparent on her face and in her voice.

Suddenly, Hanna understood for the first time why Grandfather Rockwell had held so much contempt for these two people prostrating themselves before her. They were users. They depended on someone else to make their lives okay. She loved her mother, but she had lost all respect for her, years ago. And she loved her brother, simply because he was her brother, and for no other reason. He was a spoiled little rich boy, and he loved that image of himself.

Hanna was tired of the pressure the two of them had been putting on her to get married. And even though she could barely stand either of them at times, she knew she wouldn't be the cause of them losing the only home they had ever known.

Frankly, she'd always wondered how it would be to live somewhere else. She had spent her life right here at Rockwell Place, so at times, she thought she would welcome a change. But she knew she wouldn't make that stand against them, so she decided to go with the plan that she had been quietly formulating for the right moment. That moment seemed to be upon her, so taking a deep breath, she challenged them.

"Okay, Mother, start planning the wedding. Give it your best. We'll have a wedding on my thirtieth birthday, June 17." She heard both of them suck in their breath at the same time.

"Sis, have you been holding out on us? Who's the lucky guy?" Her brother's sardonic facial expressions of just a few minutes earlier had suddenly turned to complete joy.

"That's where you come in, dear brother." Hanna's emerald green eyes filled with contempt as they perused her weakling of a brother. "You get to find the lucky guy! Find someone that will marry me in three months, and we'll have ourselves a wedding." She found great pleasure in the look of disbelief on his face. "Just do me one favor," she continued, "try to make sure he's not a serial killer, or rapist...if you get my drift."

"How am I supposed to find you someone to marry?" her astounded brother asked. "Do I run an ad in the paper that says, 'Wanted: One Groom'?"

"However you want to handle it is fine with me. It's not my problem," Hanna answered him.

"Hanna?"

"Don't start, Mother. This is what you want, isn't it? You and Will have driven me to distraction these past few months, insisting that I find someone and get married. If you think it's as easy as all of that, then you two knock yourselves out. Just tell me what time to show up, and I'll be there." And she headed for the door. But just before she left the room, she turned back to them. "I've just realized why Grandfather wanted me to be married before I could receive what he left me. He wanted me to have someone to help protect me from you two money-grabbers."

Their gaping mouths almost made her sorry for her outburst. She turned and fled the room before they could see the tears flowing down her face.

The next morning, Hanna made her way down the spiral staircase and headed toward the formal dining room for her usual bagel and cup of coffee. Cook always prepared several breakfast items and had them waiting for the family as they drifted down to start their day.

Hanna hoped against hope she would be able to start her morning alone, but as soon as she came through the door she spotted her mother sitting at the huge antique oak dining table, dramatically grasping her head in her hands. Hanna knew she was in for a long lecture.

"Good morning, Mother," she said, and sat down at the opposite end of the table, hoping to discourage any conversation. All she wanted was to eat her breakfast in peace.

"Hanna, come down here and talk with me." Hanna could tell by the whining note in her mother's voice that she might as well give in and get this over with, so, reluctantly, she gathered up her bagel and coffee and moved closer to her mother.

"Hanna, what you said yesterday really hurt me. I'm your mother, and I love you. I'm just trying to look out for you and your brother. I want what's best for you. I want us all to be able to continue living in the custom that we've always been used to. None of us know how to go out into the world and make a living."

Hanna knew when her mother used this tone of voice that there was no use trying to reason with her, so she didn't volunteer any conversation, and her mother continued.

"Maybe if you would have listened to me all these years I've tried to encourage you to lose that weight, we wouldn't be in this situation. You have such a beautiful face, and I know you would be able to find a fine young man to marry if you looked more like those models in the magazines and on TV."

There had been a time when her mother's comments would have caused Hanna to run to her room and cry for hours, then get up the next day and go on the latest fad diet. But not any more. She had long since learned to ignore her mother and Will's hard comments about her size. She had learned how to tune them out, and think about something that made her happy.

This morning, she gazed lovingly at the life-size portrait of her grandparents that hung over the large mantle at the end of the dining room, where on cold winter nights a roaring fire blazed in the huge fireplace, turning the large formal room into a warm, welcoming haven.

Even in death, it seemed her grandfather kept watch over the family from his vantage point, as he looked down on gatherings in the room he loved the most. Her grandfather stood tall and handsome, and his piercing blue eyes seemed to look into the soul of anyone looking up at the portrait. His eyes seemed to follow a person around the room, and Hanna loved that about the portrait. It almost seemed as if Grandfather was there with her.

The portrait of her grandmother could have been of Hanna, it looked so much like her. She had inherited her grandmother's golden red hair, big emerald green eyes, peaches and cream complexion, and her voluptuous body. That's why Grandfather had loved Hanna so much. She had reminded him of his beloved Victoria, whom he had lost when she gave birth to their only son, Greg, Hanna's father. And even though Hanna had never seen her grandmother, she knew more about her than most people know about their living grandmothers. Grandfather had spent hours on end, telling her stories about her grandmother.

And as her mother droned on, Hanna again memorized every detail of her grandmother's image. She was glad she looked like her, but Hanna knew she would never find a man like Grandfather, who would love her and her own voluptuous body like he had loved her grandmother. In her grandmother's day, it was considered beautiful to be well rounded. But it seemed that all the men these days were taken with Hollywood's typical size six female body, so she had given up on ever finding the man of her dreams. The man who would love her for her mind as well as her body.

"Hanna, are you listening to me?" Her mother's impatient voice interrupted her thoughts.

"Actually, I wasn't, Mother. So if you're finished, I have things to do."

"Hold on! Not so fast, I have great news!" Will burst into the room just as Hanna was about to make her exit.

Sinking slowly back into her chair, she waited to see what new scheme Will had come up with.

"Sis, I've found your future husband!" He couldn't hide the jubilation in his voice.

Hanna felt as if her insides were going to shrivel up and die. She had hoped this plan wouldn't work, but here he was, the day after she had laid down her challenge, with a prospect for her to marry. He had really spent a lot of time trying to find the man she was supposed to spend her life with, she thought ruefully. Actually, Grandfather's will hadn't specified how long she stayed married, just that she got married. She planned to get a divorce as soon as the will was settled. This farce of a marriage wouldn't last long.

"Well, don't you want to know who he is?" Will asked impatiently.

Hanna had a sudden urge to reach over and slap him in the mouth. But instead, she said, "Not really, but I can tell you're going to tell me anyway."

"Matt Corbett!" Satisfaction sounded in every word.

Laughter exploded from Hanna's throat.

"*The* Matt Corbett?" Her mother asked in awe.

"The one and the same!" Will practically shouted.

"But how? Why?" Their mother was flushed with excitement from the news.

"Oh, Mother, can't you see he's just playing one of his childish tricks on us? Surely you don't believe Matt Corbett would agree to marry someone he's never seen. With all he has going on for him, he can choose anyone he wants." Hanna's sound reasoning brought her mother back to earth.

"Well, Sis, ol' Matt has run into a little trouble with the Internal Revenue Service. It seems that his manager has been skimming off the top, bottom, and middle of Matt's finances, and hasn't been paying any of Matt's bills, so he's in big trouble. The IRS came in last week and confiscated everything he owns that's worth a dime, and Matt's about to declare bankruptcy. I just happened to find him drowning his sorrows in his beer last night, and I gave him the proposal of a lifetime. I told him I would pay off his debts if he would marry my sister, sight unseen. He agreed." Will slapped the polished oak table so hard it made both women jump.

"Will, he was drunk! I'm sure when he wakes up this morning and realizes what he's done, he'll change his mind." Hanna couldn't believe her brother was naive enough to believe Matt Corbett would marry her.

"It won't matter if he does want to change his mind," Will stated with a smug look on his face. "He's in the palm of our hands!"

"And why is that?" Hanna wondered what Will could have possibly done to be so sure of his "catch."

"As soon as he agreed to my terms, I called Carl Hardin, and took Matt to Carl's office and we drew up the papers last night. It's legal. He can't back out."

"Will, one of these days that crooked lawyer friend of yours is going to get the two of you into something he can't talk your way out of. This just may be it," Hanna warned.

Matthew Corbett came slowly awake. His mouth felt like it had a three-pound cotton ball stuck where his tongue was supposed to be. His head felt as if it would explode if he moved it at all, and when he tried to open his squinted eyes to the sun shining in through the dingy window, he gave a cry of pain and fell back on the bed.

Moving very slowly, he made himself get off the bed. He had to go to the bathroom or he was going to pee on himself. Finally, after washing his face and combing his hair, he stumbled back into the small dingy hotel room where he had spent the night.

Reality crept into his foggy brain. His house was gone. His car was gone. Hell, he barely had the money to rent this cheap hotel room for the night. And going out last night, spending money getting drunk wasn't the smartest thing he'd ever done, either. When he got a chance to find that damn manager who had screwed him out of everything, he wouldn't have to worry about a place to stay. He was going to kill that son of a bitch, and then he'd be in prison. At least he'd have a place to sleep and food to eat.

He slumped into the uncomfortable chair beside the wobbly table in the corner of the room and was about to hold his throbbing head in his hands when he spotted the papers on the table. Not remembering laying any papers on the table, he reached over and started to read the contents.

The letterhead was from a lawyer's office, and the document stated that he had agreed to marry someone named Hanna Rockwell, sight unseen, in exchange for enough money to pay off all his debts plus settle the score that was left over with the IRS if what they collected from his possessions didn't cover what he owed them.

Sight unseen? What kind of woman was she that he would have to agree to marry her "sight unseen"? Was she some kind of monster? His hangover didn't stop him from conjuring up all kinds of horror images of some woman who didn't want to be seen until after her wedding. And why did she have to have an arranged wedding? Was she so repulsive she couldn't even find her own husband?

But the worst horror of all was finding his own signature at the end of the three-page document. He had already agreed to do this! He couldn't deny his own signature scrawled in the spot marked by an X. But how? When?

He vaguely remembered some guy having a couple of drinks with him last night, but he had already been pretty far gone when the guy joined him at his table, so he didn't remember anything about him. Was he the one who had gotten up this bogus contract? He picked up the phone and called the number that was on the letterhead.

"Carl Hardin's office," a man's voice answered.

"Carl Hardin, please," Matt requested.

"Speaking."

"Carl, this is Matt Corbett. I need to talk to you about a contract I supposedly signed last night."

"Hello," Hanna spoke into the phone receiver.

"Hanna? This is Carl Hardin. Is Will there?" Hanna had never heard Carl sound so stressed before.

"Yes, he's here. Do you want to speak with him?"

"No, just tell him to get down here right now. Matt Corbett is on his way to see us."

Hanna hung up the phone and turned back to her mother and Will, who were discussing the possibilities of having Matt Corbett as part of their family.

"I do believe there's already trouble with your new business partner, Will. That was Carl. He wants you in his office right now. Seems as if a certain Matt Corbett is on his way to see you two." Hanna couldn't keep the note of victory from her voice.

Will's face turned a little white as he bounded for the door.

"Really, Hanna, I think you like making things difficult. I believe you secretly want this whole thing to fall through," her mother said, and stormed from the room.

Carrying a fresh cup of steaming coffee, Hanna opened the sliding glass doors that led from the dining room and stepped onto the adjoining deck. A cool spring breeze danced through the treetops to the music of singing birds. Leaning back in a chaise lounge, Hanna closed her eyes and reveled in the peace of the moment.

Matt Corbett. What would life be like with Matt Corbett, the rock star? Well, he used to be a rock star. She remembered when she thought he was the most handsome man who ever lived. And sexy! Her full understanding of the word "sexy" came as a result of her teenage crush on Matt Corbett.

She used to have a full size poster of him in her room. What happened to that poster? Did she still have it stored away somewhere? She would look for it later. But she didn't need a picture to remember how he looked. He was medium height, not a big man, but that dark hair and those smoky brown eyes, and that olive complexion, made him look so masculine that women made fools of themselves constantly over him. And when he was on stage, shaking his hips like he did—Hanna felt her body go warm all over.

A smile played on her full lips as she let herself fantasize briefly about being married to Matt Corbett. *She* sure wouldn't mind. She wouldn't be in as big a hurry to divorce him as she had planned on if *he* wound up being her husband.

What if it did happen? And wouldn't it be a hoot if he found her really attractive and fell in love with her, and—

"Hoooold it!" she admonished herself out loud. She wouldn't let herself get too carried away with a fantasy she knew could never happen.

But she couldn't get Matt Corbett off her mind. After several attempts to relax and enjoy the morning, she gave up and headed upstairs to see if she could find her teenage treasures. Soon she found the box where she had stored some of her old memorabilia. Standing in the far back corner of her closet was the cardboard poster of Matt.

Pulling the poster out of the closet made Hanna feel like a teenager again. Her heart pounded faster, just gazing at Matt's beautiful smile. He had been her idol. Her dream man.

In the poster he had on the tight jeans and black leather jacket that was his trademark. His dark hair was slicked back off his face, but hung to his shoulders. The guitar strap was drooped loosely around his neck and the guitar hung seductively between his legs as he stood with feet apart and hands in the air, as if he had just finished a perfect performance.

And his performances *had* been perfect. But then he started to quietly fade from the public's eye, and gradually disappeared as so many of the great performers do.

She had mourned his slow disappearance almost as one would mourn a lost lover. She had acquired any and all information about him that was available to the public. She knew his likes and dislikes.

His favorite colors. His favorite foods. She could have answered any trivia question about him that anyone could have possibly asked.

She wondered if he'd changed much in the last 15 years. Did he still wear black jeans and a black leather jacket? Did he still have that smooth, sexy voice?

She was so lost in her memories that she didn't hear Will calling her name until he was almost to her room. Hurriedly, she stood the poster back inside her closet and barely had the door closed when Will burst into her room.

"He's going to do it! He's curious as to why he can't see you until after the wedding, but Carl and I talked to him until he agreed to go through with it!"

"Will, I'm curious about that, too," Hanna interrupted him.

"What?" He looked puzzled.

"Why can't my prospective husband see me? Why did you come up with that stipulation?"

"Well—uh—I just thought—"

Will's stumbling over an excuse irritated Hanna, because she knew full well the reason he'd come up with that stipulation. He was afraid if Matt Corbett knew she was fat, he wouldn't agree to the wedding.

"Forget it, Will. Just go. I have things to do." She shooed him from her room.

After closing and locking the door behind Will, Hanna went back to the closet. She found her favorite Matt Corbett CD and stuck it into the CD player. Remembered schoolgirl emotions swept over her as his voice started crooning her favorite love song. It was one of his slower songs, which allowed the quality of his voice to come through.

She took the poster out and stood it against the wall. Suddenly Matt's eyes seemed to lock with hers, and panic washed over her. She was going to marry Matt Corbett! She was going to marry the only man she had ever had a crush on! And she was scared!

She sank slowly to the floor in front of the poster and gazed up at it. Her chest felt as if her heart would tear its way through her ribcage. Her palms started to bead up with moisture.

What was she going to do? What if she went through with this wedding and he found her repulsive? In her fantasies, he had always been the one who had loved her unconditionally. He had loved her just the way she was, and had never wanted her to starve herself and lose weight. Now that fantasy was going to be blown.

She couldn't let that happen. She would just stick with her initial plan. She would go through with the wedding, and then she would disappear until the will was settled. Then she would get a divorce. She would arrange it to where Matt Corbett would never see her, except on their wedding day. That way, she would never have to see the disappointment in his eyes when he realized what she looked like.

With that decision made, Hanna could feel herself start to calm down. She stood the poster in the closet, but left it where she could see it when the door was open. She could dream, even if nothing would ever come of those dreams.

Sunday morning when Hanna came down for breakfast, her mother already had the Sunday paper spread out on the dining room table. Good, Hanna thought. Maybe if her mother was reading, she wouldn't start babbling about Matt Corbett like she had done continually since Will had announced that Matt had, indeed, agreed to the wedding contract.

Hanna had her usual cup of coffee and bagel, and was contentedly nibbling the raisins off the bagel when she heard her mother's sharply in-drawn breath.

13

"Oh—my—word!" She screeched, half rising from her chair.

"Mother, what is it?" Hanna asked, giving her mother her complete attention for a change.

But all her mother could do was point at the paper.

In exasperation, Hanna got up and went to read what her mother was pointing at. There on the front of the "Living" section of the paper was a large picture of Hanna, with a headline reading *Rockwell Heiress Finally Sets the Date.*

Hanna stared open-mouthed at the photo. It was a recent picture that had been taken one day when she had gone to the park for a brief getaway from Rockwell Place. One of the local TV crews was out filming "first signs of spring," as they called it. She had been standing beside a huge old oak tree, watching the squirrels, when a young photographer had walked up to her and asked if he could take her picture. She had agreed, but had asked him not to put it on TV.

She'd had on a cream-colored chiffon dress that reached to her ankles, and the wind had it plastered against her body. Her hair had been whipped into a mass of reddish golden curls that seemed to be everywhere at once. Hanna smiled to herself. The young photographer was really good. He'd made her look like a sex goddess from some other century.

"I'll sue that stupid paper. Look what they've done to you! They've made you look like some wanton floozy! I'm calling them right now!"

"No, Mother. You aren't going to call or to sue." Determination sounded in Hanna's every word. Seldom did she stand up to her mother, but when she did, she usually got results.

"But why? We didn't give them permission to print this. They can't print something like this without asking us first." Frustration sounded in every word.

"Who have you told about the wedding?"

"Well—I—uh—well—a lot of people," her mother stuttered.

"I know. I've heard you on the phone constantly talking about it," Hanna said, accusingly.

"But I have to make plans. I can't plan a wedding without talking about it."

"Did you speak with Mrs. Tolbert?"

"Yes," her mother said. "I asked her to tell the bridge club I wouldn't be there for a few weeks. I would be busy with the wedding."

"And did she ask about photos for the paper?" Hanna persisted.

"Yes, she asked if I had any pictures of you. I told her I didn't have any good ones." Her mother didn't even consider how her statement might make Hanna feel.

"And? What did she say?"

"Hmmmmm. Oh, she asked if I did have a good picture, would I agree to let the paper run an article about the wedding. I told her I would, and she asked a few more questions, and that was all of the conversation."

"Well, Mother, that was how the picture got into the paper. Tom, the photographer who took the picture, is Mrs. Tolbert's son. He does freelance photography for the paper and TV stations."

"But still, I didn't give them permission."

"Forget it, Mother. It's my picture. If anyone has a right to have a problem it should be me, and I don't have a problem with it."

"But it makes you look so—so—"

"Fat?" Hanna filled in the word she knew her mother was trying so hard not to say.

"Well, I didn't say that!"

"No, but you wanted to," Hanna said, and, taking her bagel and coffee, escaped to the balcony.

Matt Corbett perched on a stool in front of the counter at the little coffee shop two blocks from the motel where Will Rockwell had paid his expenses until the wedding. He ordered coffee and a sweet roll from the waitress, who kept flirting with him every chance she got.

He wasn't totally broke, but his assets were frozen until he could get this IRS fiasco straightened out. So Will had also given him a food allowance until the wedding. He didn't like Will Rockwell much. He couldn't figure out the guy's motives. Why was he in such a hurry to get his sister married off, and why couldn't Matt see his future wife? He had an occasional nightmare of lifting the veil to kiss his new bride and finding a snake's head in place of a woman's.

He couldn't believe what a mess his life had gotten into. How in the hell had he, Matt Corbett, come to the point in his life that he was having to depend on a rich playboy to support him until he could say "I do" to the playboy's mysterious sister?

He probably could have gotten out of the contract he'd signed when he was dog drunk, but the next day at the lawyer's office Will and the lawyer had been so persuasive, he'd decided to give it a shot. After all, what did he have to lose? His career was sure shot to hell. His band had long since broken up and each member had found another gig to pull. And now that the government had confiscated all his possessions, he had absolutely nothing. He should be thankful that something like this Rockwell situation had come along when it did. Where would he be without it? On the streets, probably. Of course, the IRS didn't give a damn about that as long as they got theirs.

But the mysterious bride-to-be bothered him a lot. Would he be expected to perform sexually? Just like a real husband? There had been nothing in the contract about that.

Weary from trying to figure it all out, Matt reached for the Sunday paper someone had left lying on the counter. The "Living" section was on top. As he pulled the paper toward him he was captivated by a picture of a gorgeous woman that covered most of the page. Whoever had taken the photograph was good. They'd captured the golden highlights in her light red hair. They'd captured the creamy complexion and those big green eyes.

Matt's eyes traveled down her body. The wind had pressed her dress against her, outlining her large breasts and full hips. It even revealed the V between her legs. Now here was a woman! She almost looked like a goddess from a long-lost island. One that he would like to be stranded on, if she was there, he mused with a lopsided grin.

At 36, Matt had reached a place in his life where he was secure enough in his manhood that he wasn't afraid anymore to admit he liked women with a little meat on their bones. He had spent years trying to make himself feel attracted to the skinny women that were splashed everywhere he looked, but he finally realized he just wasn't attracted to that type of woman. He knew a lot of men who were, or who said they were, and to each his own, but he had "come out."

He was no longer a closet lover of big beautiful women. He loved them right out in the open, and it felt so good. He had been amazed when some of his friends gladly agreed with him when he stated his preference for larger women. It was almost like they had been afraid to be the first to admit they felt the same way.

But why couldn't he have met someone like this gorgeous babe before he agreed to marry "the monster lady," as he had taken to calling her in his mind? Did the paper give her name? Maybe he'd call her if she weren't married. If this goddess was available, he might have to call off this farce of a marriage.

Then his eyes fell on the headline, *Rockwell Heiress Finally Sets the Date.* Realization didn't sink in when he first read the words. So what's her name, he wondered, looking for the article that went with the picture. Then it hit him.

"*Rockwell?*" He didn't realize he'd spoken out loud. Could this be?

Frantically, he searched for the article.

> *Hanna Rockwell, heiress to the Rockwell Place estate, has set her wedding date. According to sources, unless Hanna marries by her 30th birthday, she and her family lose the entire estate. The wedding will take place on June 17.*

So that's it! Suddenly, the mystery cleared up. Brother Will had to find his sister a husband or the family would lose their estate.

But why wasn't Matt allowed to see her? That didn't make any sense. And why couldn't a woman who looked like that picture find a husband on her own? Why did her brother have to get a total stranger to sign a contract to marry her sight unseen? Was there something else wrong with her? Something that didn't show up in this picture? Was she mentally unstable? Solving the mystery of finding out how she looked just seemed to add more questions for him.

But looking again at the picture in front of him, suddenly Matt didn't care. She was beautiful! He laughed out loud as he picked up the paper, stuck it under his arm and left the coffee shop.

Life had suddenly taken on a whole new meaning.

Chapter 2

Hanna watched as the sun slowly started to stream in through the sheer curtains, causing bright highlights to dance across the room where she had spent her childhood. She had always loved waking up in this room each morning. Even on cloudy days, the room was bright and cheery.

She had spent a restless, sleepless night, just waiting, dreading for the sun to rise. It was June 17. Her 30th birthday. Her wedding day.

She faced the day with mixed emotions. On the one hand, she was glad all the preparations were finally over. Her mother had driven her to distraction with the continuous search for the "perfect" wedding gown, the "perfect" decorations, and the "perfect" guest list. In actuality, this was her mother's wedding. Only Hanna would be the bride, and not her mother.

So for that reason, Hanna had taken little interest in the preparations. And this had frustrated her mother beyond reason. But why should Hanna care? This wasn't a real wedding. She knew she would probably never have a real wedding. So why should she worry about all the to-do over nothing?

She was just a tool in her mother's quest to make an impression on her high-society snobbish friends. Hanna had contemplated walking down the isle nude, just to spite her mother.

Hanna dreaded the day and what it held because it would end life, as she knew it, for a while. She glanced at the closet, thinking about the packed luggage tucked in the far end, out of sight. She mentally went over each item again, just to make sure she had packed everything.

As soon as the ceremony was over and she came back to her room to change, she would call a cab and then go down the fire escape outside her window, heading for Grandfather's hunting cabin, tucked away in the woods of East Tennessee. She had been there with him on many occasions, and knew the cabin was stocked with enough supplies to last her for a good while.

And besides that, a small town was within easy driving from the cabin. Hanna could go for supplies any time she needed something.

She would leave a note to her mother, letting her know she was going away for a while, so she wouldn't worry. But Hanna wasn't telling anyone where she was going. Once she got settled in, she would call the family lawyer, Houston Couch, and give him her cell phone number so he could keep her informed about the settling of the will. She knew she could persuade Houston to keep her location a secret from her mother and Will. Houston had known Grandfather well, and knew the family situation. She could count on him to hastily settle the will, then just as hastily proceed with the divorce arrangements.

Hanna's mind drifted to the poster of Matt Corbett that still stood inside her closet. Every time she thought of him, her heart beat faster. Would he still look like he did when he'd been a rock star? She knew he was six years older than her, so he would be 36, now. Was his hair turning gray? Maybe he had changed so much he wouldn't even look like the same person that she'd had such a crush on as a teenager.

What would he think of her? She had to admit, her mother had picked the most perfect wedding dress of all the ones Hanna had tried on. A princess-style design, it fit her body snugly and enhanced her hourglass figure. The bodice dipped just low enough to show a modest amount of cleavage. The hemline ended just above the floor, and a long flowing train trailed behind. The veil was thin and almost transparent, and gave Hanna a mysterious appeal. She never admitted it to her mother, but Hanna felt exquisite in the dress. But after all, all brides were beautiful. At least that's what she'd always heard.

The morning passed quickly, and much too soon Hanna stood in front of the floor length mirror in the dressing room of the church. As the bridesmaids *ooh'ed* and *aah'ed* over her, she gazed at her reflection. She did look beautiful, she admitted to herself. Her eyes sparkled with the excitement of the moment, and to anyone who didn't know, she looked like a real bride, about to face the man she loved and wanted to spend the rest of her life with.

Suddenly, she wished Grandfather could be here to see her and give her away at her wedding, even if it wasn't a real wedding. But, of course, if Grandfather were here, there wouldn't be a wedding.

Grandfather had been more like a father to her than a grandfather. Hanna's father had been killed in a one-car accident when she was two years old, and she couldn't remember him at all. Having

Grandfather around all her life had made it easier to cope with not having a father.

The nervous shuffling of the women in the room with her brought Hanna out of her reverie, and she realized the music had started. It was time.

Her mother came hurrying into the room to make a last-minute check on her project. She inspected Hanna carefully.

"Hanna," she started hesitantly, looking deeply into Hanna's eyes. "I realize what you're doing is a great sacrifice, and I just want you to know that I appreciate it. You're my daughter and I love you. You look beautiful today."

A compliment from Mary Rockwell was a rare thing. Surprised at her mother's unusual show of sincerity and affection, Hanna smiled at her and lightly kissed her cheek.

"Thanks for that, Mama." She briefly wondered how much better their relationship would have been down through the years if her mother had shown this side of her nature more often.

Will was waiting for her at the door to the auditorium. He would be the one to give her away. How ironic, Hanna thought. He desperately needed her inheritance, and assumed he would be in better financial shape once the estate was Hanna's. He had found her a willing groom, so the stipulations of the will would be satisfied, and now he would happily lead her down the isle and hand her over to a stranger, just so his life would be better.

As she stopped beside him and placed her hand on his arm, he whispered, "Wow, I guess it's true that all brides are beautiful. Even you look beautiful today."

But Hanna didn't acknowledge him. Her eyes had found the man standing at the end of the isle waiting to become her husband. Her heart leaped into her throat when she found and recognized Matt Corbett. Much to her dismay, from this distance he didn't look like he had changed a bit. The only difference in the way he looked now was that he had on a black tuxedo instead of a black leather jacket. But everything else about him looked the same as it had all those years ago when she watched him on stage and swooned along with all the other teenage girls in the audience.

She had hoped he'd changed enough that she wouldn't be constantly reminded of who he was and how she used to feel about him. Even from this distance he seemed to exude a masculine strength that made her knees start to shake.

As the bridal march began and she slowly made her way towards her new life, Hanna was oblivious to the guests watching her make her way down the isle. She watched the face of Matt Corbett. His eyes slowly looked her over, then finally came back to hers and locked.

Hanna felt herself stumble slightly and knew her hands must be shaking, for Will suddenly tightened the muscles in the arm her hand rested on, pressing her hand close to his side, and leaned down to her to whisper, "Matt's really a nice guy. I've talked to him quite a lot in the past few days. I think you'll like him."

Hanna mentally thanked Will for his brief concern, but she never took her eyes off Matt's. She didn't seem able to. And as she drew closer to him, she imagined she saw golden flecks dancing in his eyes, and she imagined she saw something else. Something that looked almost like admiration.

One thing she knew. She didn't see the revulsion that she had expected when he realized she wasn't a size six.

Shyness overtook her when she placed her hand on his arm, and, unable to look into his eyes, she turned to face the minister. Matt turned slightly toward her and placed his hand over hers. Surprised, she looked up into his direct gaze. She hadn't imagined the golden flecks. They were there like a warm fire, and she felt heat spread through her body.

He wasn't much taller than Hanna, and she briefly thought how easy it would be to kiss him. Flustered at her own thoughts, she looked quickly back at the minister who had started the ceremony, but she was keenly aware that Matt Corbett never took his eyes from her face.

She felt lightheaded, as if she might faint. What was going on? This wasn't going at all as she had expected. She hadn't wanted to see contempt on his face, but she hadn't expected this heated light in his eyes, either. Almost as if he found her attractive.

"Hanna, do you take Matt to be your lawfully wedded husband?" The minister's kindly expression made Hanna realize he'd probably asked the question already, and she hadn't heard him.

"I do," she whispered, barely loud enough to be heard.

"And, Matt, do you take Hanna to be your lawfully wedded wife?"

"I do," Matt's voice was strong and sincere, and again, Hanna found herself captured in his gaze.

"Will you be exchanging rings?" The minister asked.

Hanna, not having thought of such a thing, was surprised when someone handed Matt a ring. She watched in amazement as he took her hand and slipped a wide gold band on her finger. It fit as if it had been made for her.

"It was my mother's," Matt said softly. "It's all I could afford right now," he added almost apologetically. His voice sounded low and sensual, just like it did when he sang his slow love songs.

Hanna looked at the ring on her hand. His mother's? He'd given her, a total stranger, his mother's wedding band?

"Hanna!" She realized Will was pressing something in her palm, and, looking down, found a gold band in her hand. Glancing quickly at Will, she realized the ring was for Matt and she was expected to put it on him. Her hands shook so hard, she barely got the ring on him without dropping it.

"I now pronounce you man and wife. You may kiss the bride." The minister concluded the ceremony.

Matt was raising her veil. She hadn't planned on this! She wanted desperately to grasp the veil and pull it back down. The veil had been her protection, her security, and now it was being slowly lifted.

She stood immobilized and watched Matt Corbett's face, waiting to see his expression change. Waiting for some clue that he suddenly realized what he had done. Waiting for anything but the easy, sensual smile that spread across his chiseled lips. "You are beautiful," he whispered, lowering his mouth to hers.

Hanna was shaken to the depth of her soul when Matt's lips covered hers. The kiss wasn't a simple "just for appearances" peck, but a real kiss. She felt his tongue gently trace the outline of her full lips. Her lips parted of their own accord, to allow him to deepen the kiss.

"Okay, children, that's enough." Someone brought them back to the present.

Dazed, Hanna allowed Matt to lead her back down the isle. She heard, as if from a great distance, people saying how beautiful she looked, and how handsome the groom was. Once outside the church, people started throwing birdseed at them, and Matt hurriedly escorted Hanna to the waiting limousine.

Once safely inside, Hanna leaned back against the seat and breathed a long sigh.

"Hello, I'm Matthew Corbett." Matt said, leaning over and offering her his outstretched hand.

Hanna placed her hand in his and was about to introduce herself when the irony of the situation overcame her, and she broke into near hysterical laughter.

Matt joined in with her laughter, and Hanna could feel the tension start to drain from her.

Suddenly, she wanted to ask Matt Corbett a thousand questions. And suddenly, she was sorry she'd made plans to disappear after her wedding. She realized now she might enjoy becoming friends with Matt Corbett, since he hadn't reacted at all like she'd expected him to. But it was too late for that now. They would soon be home, and she would disappear, and he would be gone from her life when she returned.

Glancing out the window of the limo to see how close they were to being home, Hanna realized they weren't on the street that led to Rockwell Place. She tapped on the dividing partition to get the driver's attention. He slid the partition open.

"Henri, where are we headed?" Hanna asked. "You're supposed to be taking us home."

"Not according to Mr. Couch," Henri said, shaking his head. "He told me to bring you straight to the airport."

"To the airport? For what?" Suddenly angry, Hanna suspected her mother had a hand in what was going on. "Do you know what's going on?" She asked Matt.

"No, Hanna, I know nothing," Matt assured her. She loved the way her name sounded on his lips.

"Henri, go home, right this minute," she demanded of the driver.

"Miss—uh—Mrs. Hanna, I can't do that. Mr. Couch told me not to let you harass me into doing anything except bring you and Mr. Corbett straight to the airport, and that's what I'm doing. You can take it up with him once we get there." And Henri closed the partition so he couldn't hear Hanna's protests.

Frustrated, Hanna slammed her body back against the seat.

"Damn them," she said out loud. "They got what they wanted. I got married for them, now why can't they just get out of my life for a change and leave me alone." She had momentarily forgotten she wasn't alone in the big car.

"Hanna," Matt said, sliding across the seat, closer to her, "Will got slightly tipsy the other night and told me your whole situation. In fact, he was a little more than tipsy. He was basically drunk, and as far as I could tell, he pretty much spilled his guts about your family, according to how he sees it, going back as far as he could remember. So if there is anything you need to talk about, I'm a good listener."

But Hanna didn't want to talk. She just wanted to get to the airport and find out what her mother and Will had done now.

"Thanks, but I don't guess there's anything to talk about." She couldn't hide the slight trace of sadness in her voice.

"Hanna, the only thing I couldn't get Will to tell me was why I couldn't see you before we got married. I still can't figure it out. What was that all about?"

Hanna looked deeply into Matt's eyes. He seemed so sincere! Had he really not realized the obvious reason Will wanted to keep her hidden?

"In case you haven't noticed, I'm not a size six. Will was afraid you wouldn't go along with the deal if you saw that you were going to have a fat wife." Her smile trembled on her full lips, and a tear rolled down her cheek. Hating to appear weak and self-pitying, Hanna reached to wipe the tear away, but Matt stopped her hand. He gently wiped the tear away with his thumb, then trailed his hand down her cheek.

"Your brother's a fool," he whispered softly, and covered her lips with his in a gentle, probing kiss.

Not wanting to, but unable to stop herself, Hanna parted her lips to allow the kiss to deepen. This kind of wantonness was totally alien to her, but Matt's tenderness had overcome her, robbing her of the strength to stop the wonderful sensations he was stirring in her.

Hanna was brought back to reality by the limousine slowing to a stop. Flushed and flustered, she exited the limousine, feeling self-conscious about looking like a fresh-kissed bride. But she soon realized most of the attention was on Matt, as people recognized him as he walked past. Henri led them to an office on the ground floor of the airport, and knocked softly on the door.

Houston Couch opened the door and smiled at Henri. "Thanks, Henri. I wondered if you'd make it or not." He motioned for Hanna and Matt to come inside.

Hanna wasn't surprised to find her mother and Will sitting on a couch that lined one side of the room.

Houston motioned for Hanna and Matt to sit down.

"Hanna, I know you're wondering what's going on, so I'm going to get right to the reason I had Henri bring you here. This is phase two of your grandfather's will."

"Phase two?" Hanna, her mother, and Will chorused at the same time.

"Yes. Mr. Rockwell has left instructions for three phases. It seems he was afraid Hanna would be railroaded into getting married just to save the estate, so he has tried to assure that she not only got married, but that she was in a happy marriage."

Someone groaned out loud, and Hanna realized it was her. Why had Grandfather complicated her life like this? What could he have possibly been thinking?

"Mr. Rockwell," Houston was continuing, "wanted to insure that his name and lineage would continue with Hanna. He wanted to make sure she wasn't railroaded— " He used the word again, each time looking directly at Mary and Will as he said it— "into hastily marrying someone just to get the money, then divorcing the man as soon as the estate was in place."

"Okay," Will said impatiently, "what is phase two?"

"Phase two is a honeymoon that your grandfather," Houston continued, looking at Hanna, "has planned in detail, with monies set aside for each segment of the honeymoon."

"And what is phase three?" Hanna asked, afraid of the answer.

"Hanna, don't you want to wait until the honeymoon is over?" Houston asked.

"What is phase three?" Hanna asked again, through clenched teeth.

"Phase three, and the completion of the will, will happen when you're expecting a baby." Houston Couch wouldn't meet Hanna's horror-stricken eyes.

"NO!" she shouted. "You take that will right now and shred the damn thing. And if you have any idea how to contact my dead grandfather, tell him I hope he's burning in hell for this!"

"Hanna, calm down!" Her mother shouted. "You can't seriously mean what you said."

"Hanna, you can't give up now," Will whined. "We've already gotten through the hardest part."

"We? And what do you mean the hardest part?" Hanna ground out.

"Well, finding someone who would marry you, sight unseen, like you are and everything." In his excitement, Will forgot to be careful of his words.

Suddenly, Matt stood and grabbed Will's tie and pulled him to a half standing position. "As long as I'm married to your sister, you will respect her. Do you understand me?" Matt gave Will a slight shake to get his point across. Will's air was cut off, so all he could do was nod his head in agreement.

Matt shoved Will roughly back into his seat, and sat back down beside Hanna.

"Hanna," Houston Couch began again, coughing behind his hand to cover a smile, "Your grandfather loved you dearly, but he was afraid you would allow those around you to use you for the money he was leaving you. He stated his concerns to me many times before he died. He wished more than anything that you could find a good strong man to walk through life with you, supporting and caring for you. I believe you may have found him." He smiled again at the memory of Matt choking Will's air off.

"Mrs. Rockwell," Houston continued, "you and Will wait for me outside, please. I need to have a private conversation with Hanna and Matt. I'll be with you shortly."

When the door had closed behind the two people who had reluctantly left the room, Houston turned to Hanna.

"What I'm about to show you is for your eyes only. Yours and your husband's." He put a tape into a VCR in a corner of the room.

To Hanna's amazement, Grandfather's face appeared on the screen, and he started talking directly to her.

"Hanna, if you're watching this, then I'm no longer with you. I hope you're having a good life.

"You know I've only wanted the best for you. I hope none of the things I've done have made you feel angry with me, because I've only done them to protect you, and what I've left you. You know I've never cared for your mother, but I always let her remain at my house for your sake. What I'm about to tell you, is strictly confidential, and for you to use only as you see fit.

"William is only your half brother. I had a suspicion that your mother was cheating on my son, so when William was born, I insisted that blood tests be done, and sure enough, he wasn't your father's child. Your father declared his love for your mother anyway, so I didn't have the heart to throw her out, because I knew my son would follow her, and possibly be lost to me forever.

"When you were born, I had more blood tests run. You were your father's child. My true grandchild. I tried early on to forget the past and treat William as if he were my grandson, but the older he got and the more your mother spoiled him, I just turned more and more away from him.

"As far as I know, he isn't aware that he isn't a blood Rockwell. I promised your father I wouldn't tell him. I do think William has the right to know who he

33

is, though, for health records and such. If the time ever comes that he needs to know, or you decide he needs to know, and your mother isn't around to tell him, all the answers you need are in a safety deposit box in the bank.

"Hanna, I'm telling you this so you'll understand why I've had to go to such lengths to protect your rightful heritage. You are the only true Rockwell left in our immediate family, after I'm gone. So honor what I've left you. Enjoy it, and pass it on to your children. I always dreamed of seeing my great grandchildren, but you didn't move as fast in that direction as I moved in the direction where I am now, so my great grandchildren and I have passed along the way without seeing each other.

"If for some reason you can't have children, leave the money where you think it will do the best work. I worked hard to acquire and keep what I'm leaving you. Take care of it.

"And remember, Hanna, I have loved you more than anyone on this earth except your grandmother. Hopefully, I'm with her now. Have a good life, Hanna."

By the time the tape was finished, Hanna was weeping quietly into a tissue Matt had handed her from a box on the desk.

Finally, after the tears had subsided, Hanna looked at Houston. "I thought the will wouldn't be complete until I got pregnant. Grandfather said on the tape to pass the money on if I didn't have children."

"I left part of the stipulations out until we were alone. Your grandfather specified in the will that if for some reason you couldn't have children, to release the estate to you in full. And actually, he specified if you didn't have children by the time you were thirty-five, to release the estate to you in full."

"Why did Grandfather specify that I had to be married by the time I was 30, or the estate would go to charity?" Hanna asked.

"Your grandfather was afraid that if you weren't married by the time you were 30, then you might have met an untimely death like your dad. He was just trying to protect his estate from the people he knew would squander it, if it fell into their hands."

Hanna's head felt as if it would explode from all the happenings of the day. She just wanted to go somewhere alone and try to digest it all. The most unsettling news of the day, though, was that Will wasn't a Rockwell.

"Houston, who is Will's father?" Hanna asked. "Do you know?"

"Henri," came Houston's one-word answer.

"Our chauffeur, Henri?" Hanna asked in disbelief.

"The one and the same. Hanna, Henri and your mother have loved each other for years. I'm surprised you haven't picked up on it."

Hanna stared at the man who had been the family lawyer for as long as she could remember. He seemed to know much more about her life than she did.

"Your grandfather knew it all along, but couldn't convince your father. As I'm sure you know, your father left the house one cold winter night, after an argument with your grandfather about the situation. Ice had formed on the bridges and overpasses, and your father hit a slick spot and ran off the road. He was traveling at a high rate of speed. He hit a tree, and was dead when the rescue squad got to him."

Hanna glanced at Matt, who sat listening, intrigued.

"Well, there's nothing like hearing about a person's entire life in a matter of hours, huh," she said, wondering what he thought about all this. He probably wished he had run far, far away that first night he and Will met.

Shrugging his shoulders, Matt chuckled and said, "At least it isn't boring."

"What are you going to do with the information about Will?" Houston asked Hanna.

"Nothing, at this point," she said. "I just wonder what Mother and Henri have in mind. If they really do love each other, I can't believe they plan to live the rest of their lives apart like they're living now."

"Are they really living apart?" Houston asked. "When was the last time you went to your mother's room in the middle of the night?"

"No! You can't be serious!" Hanna's eyes were huge with disbelief.

"Yes, I'm serious. According to your grandfather, this has been going on for years. Every night after the lights go out, Henri goes to her room and spends the night.

"But that's enough for now. You kids are going to miss your flight if we keep sitting here talking. I haven't even given you your itinerary."

"Houston, is there any way we can get out of going on a honeymoon?" Hanna asked.

"Yes," Houston said. "Again, I didn't want to say too much until we were alone, but your grandfather stated that if you preferred not to go on a honeymoon at the time of your wedding, the allotted monies would be included in the final settlement. But your mother said your bags were packed, so we assumed you planned to go on one." The lawyer looked puzzled.

"My bags were packed," Hanna said, glancing wryly at Matt, "because I was going to run away to Grandfather's hunting lodge in East Tennessee, as soon as the wedding was over. I was going to

36

hide, contact you to proceed with the finalizing of the will, and then as soon as it was all done, I was going to start divorce proceedings. But," she said, taking a deep breath, "it seems all of that has been changed, so there's no reason for me to run away."

Chapter 3

Hanna stood and watched the guests gathering in the large living room at Rockwell Place. After finding out that Hanna and Matt weren't going on a honeymoon, her mother had instantly started to plan a wedding reception. Even through it was the day after the wedding, Hanna was amazed at how many people responded to Mary Rockwell's bidding.

Hanna wore a light blue chiffon dress that flowed with each step she took, yet managed to enhance her voluptuous curves. Occasionally she could feel Matt's eyes on her, and she would turn to find him watching her. His smile or wink would send tiny tremors up her spine and she could feel the color stealing into her face. Was this something that just came naturally to him? Did he just have a way of making a woman feel beautiful, or did he really find her attractive?

She could still feel the kiss they had shared in the limo. She was still shaken at how she had responded to the kiss. But, after all, this was Matt Corbett. How could she not have responded to him?

She casually sipped a cup of punch as she watched Matt's warm response to the people her mother had invited to the wedding reception.

Almost everyone knew who Matt Corbett was, and continually congratulated her mother on her new son-in-law. Mary Rockwell was at the height of happiness, surrounded by all the high society people she had invited.

Hanna was having a hard time absorbing all that Houston Couch had told her. Especially the part about Will not being a Rockwell. Her eyes found Will across the room and watched him flirt with the group of women surrounding him. What would he do if he found out he wasn't a Rockwell? That he was just an impostor in all of this and his real father was the chauffeur? The thought caused a small smile to play around the corners of her mouth.

"Can a smile like that mean anything but trouble?" The softly spoken words at her shoulder startled Hanna.

She looked up into the eyes of her new husband. Just being this close to him was causing new and strange sensations to flood her body. The scent of his aftershave titillated her senses, sending images of lovemaking through her head.

"I think they're all waiting for us to lead them in the first dance," he said. "Shall we start the festivities?"

Setting her cup on the table she was standing beside, Hanna placed her hand into his and let him lead her to the designated dance area. As if on cue, the band started playing a waltz.

Matt slid his arms around Hanna's waist and pulled her close. They started to sway to the music.

She laid her head on his shoulder and for a moment allowed herself to live a fantasy that had been hers for years—to dance with

Matt Corbett. To feel her body pressed close to his. To feel his cheek as it rested against her hair. To feel the heat emanating from his body, warming her to a feverish pitch. To feel the pulse in his neck, pounding rapidly with the pent up passion he felt for her—

Slowly, Hanna opened her eyes enough to watch the pulse at the side of Matt's neck. This wasn't a fantasy. But his pulse was pounding, just like it had in her dreams. Could Matt actually be excited about having her in his arms?

No, she convinced herself, just as the music stopped.

Matt tried to read the morning paper, but his mind kept drifting. Little had he known, three months ago when he moved to Nashville, Tennessee to try to revive his music career, that he would wind up losing almost everything he had, personally, but would end up married to a beautiful, wealthy woman and living in a mansion like the one surrounding him now.

He glanced appreciatively around the huge, formal dining room. He assumed the portraits of the couple hanging on the wall were Hanna's grandparents. Hanna was a walking likeness of the woman in the portrait.

Upon arriving at Rockwell Place after the wedding, he'd been assigned to a guest room and told to make himself at home. He'd seen little of Hanna until the reception yesterday, much to his disappointment. That had answered the question of whether this was a marriage in name only.

The reception. A soft smile bracketed the corners of his mouth. He had never held a woman in his arms who felt as sexy as Hanna had when they'd danced yesterday. He could feel himself becoming aroused, just feeling her soft, womanly curves pressed against him. If the music hadn't stopped when it did, he would have had an embarrassing moment or two. And he could still feel her soft, full lips yielding to his when he had kissed her after the wedding.

Matt Corbett knew he had found the woman of his dreams. It was just too bad he had to find her under these circumstances. But he would get back on his feet. He would revive his music career. He would find a way to reclaim his lost success. And he would claim Hanna Rockwell as his wife.

The latter of his plans would probably be the hardest to accomplish.

Hanna glanced one last time in the mirror before heading downstairs. She knew her mother and Will would notice the extra attention she'd paid to herself this morning, but she didn't care. She was pleased with her efforts.

As soon as she came through the dining room door, she spotted Matt at the table reading the paper. A partial cup of coffee sat close to him. A smile played around his beautiful mouth.

Remembering what he had said to her the day before at the reception, Hanna repeated, "Can a smile like that mean anything but trouble?"

Matt lowered the paper to look at Hanna.

She wore a loose-fitting silk pantsuit in a deep shade of purple. Her hair was twisted into a knot on top of her head, escaping tendrils framing her face. The white open-toed sandals exposed beautifully polished toenails. Again, he felt the stirring in his lower abdomen.

"If you could read my mind right now, you might be afraid of the answer to that question." Matt stood and laid his paper down, and pulled out a chair close to him. "Here, sit down, and let me get you some coffee."

Too surprised to argue, Hanna lowered herself slowly into the chair.

Just as Matt sat the coffee down in front of her, Will and Mary came into the room.

"Oh, look, Mother, she already has him waiting on her," Will said in his usual morning bad mood. "I guess you'll just get bigger than ever, if you don't even have to wait on yourself." He looked at Hanna in disgust.

Suddenly Matt was around the table, in front of Will. "If you ever say anything like that to Hanna again, I'll beat the hell out of you, Will. I mean it. Your sister has sacrificed her happiness for you and your mother, and by damn, it's time you paid her a little respect. And as long as I'm here, you're going to do just that! Do you understand me?" he ground out.

"Look, you deadbeat—" Will started.

"Will Rockwell, sit down and shut up!"

Everyone looked at Mary at the same time.

"Will, please, just let it go," she said in a calmer voice.

Will turned and stomped from the room, leaving a hushed silence behind.

"Will doesn't mean anything bad when he talks like that." Her mother made a weak effort to defend her spoiled son. "We're just concerned about Hanna's health," she ended, lamely.

"Like hell, he doesn't mean anything," Matt snapped. Hanna was still reeling from Matt's first outburst, and couldn't believe her ears when he now turned on her mother. "Hanna looks very healthy to me. The only thing wrong with Hanna is she lets the two of you talk to her like you do. She needs to stand up for herself more." He gave Hanna a pointed look as he finished.

"You're right, of course," Mary said, dropping her head as if ashamed. "But please, let's don't argue. Let's have breakfast and talk about pleasant things. Tell us about your music days, Matt."

Hanna watched Matt deliberately calm himself down as her mother played the perfect hostess. Her mother could relax now. Her daughter was married to a handsome, well known man. Her future was secure, and she had the bragging rights of being Matt Corbett's mother-in-law.

Hanna tried to imagine her mother with Henri. Henri Dupri was a nice-looking man, about her mother's age. His slight French accent gave him a mysterious air, and Hanna could see how he could be intriguing to her mother. Had their affair started before her parents were married, or after? How long had her mother known Henri?

Suddenly Hanna realized just how much of a stranger her mother was to her. She had spent very little time with her as a child.

"Hanna," her mother's voice interrupted her thoughts, "why don't you show Matt the grounds? He might enjoy the gardens. It really is beautiful out there this time of the morning."

"That sounds like a great idea!" Matt's voice was so eager, Hanna almost broke into laughter. He was ready to escape her mother.

Hanna and Matt strolled through the lush gardens that had been her grandfather's pride and joy. They passed several people busy pruning, weeding, and doing general maintenance. Finally they came to one of Hanna's favorites, the rose garden. There were hundreds of different varieties, and the scent that greeted them was heavenly.

Hanna leaned over to sniff a beautiful yellow rose. When she lifted her eyes she caught Matt's gaze, and heat rose in her cheeks.

"Where's your favorite spot in the garden?" he asked, holding her gaze.

Hanna hesitated. Should she show him her favorite place in the whole world? It was her getaway. Her place of solitude. She doubted Will or her mother even remembered it was there. Only Grandfather knew how much the place meant to her.

"Promise you won't be a pest and try to claim it for your own?" she asked, teasingly.

"Boy Scout's honor," Matt promised, saluting with the wrong fingers and making Hanna giggle.

Wondering if she was making the right decision, she led him through the garden down a secluded stone pathway. After a few twists and turns, they came to an opening. Up a slight incline stood a little white gazebo, butted close to a rock wall.

"This is where I solve all the world's mysteries," Hanna said, and led the way up to the gazebo.

The gazebo snuggled so closely to the rock wall that it almost touched it. Within an arm's reach, a small gurgling stream of water bubbled from the rock, landing in a small smooth bowl-like cutout in the stone, then trickling down the wall to form a tiny stream running past the gazebo.

"Grandfather showed me this when I was a very small child. He said he thought Indians might have carved out the bowl to catch water. I loved the place so much and asked him to bring me here so often, he built this gazebo for us to sit in when we came. I've always loved it here. Since Grandfather died, I come here when I get lonely to be with him. He always seems nearer when I'm here." Her eyes sparkled as she reminisced.

"You really loved your grandfather, didn't you?" Matt watched the emotions play on Hanna's face as she remembered her beloved grandfather.

"Yes," Hanna answered, quietly. "He was all I had. Mother was busy spoiling Will, and now I understand why. She must have felt awfully sorry for him, knowing he would never really stand to inherit any of the properties that Grandfather would someday pass on. She must have resented me a lot, knowing in her own mind that I would get it all."

"But why? You're her child, too. What difference does it make to her who gets it, as long as she gets what she wants? She seems like the kind of woman who cares only about herself." Matt's disapproval sounded in his voice.

"I don't know. Mother and I just never have been close. As far back as I can remember, she was always trying to come up with weight loss tactics for me. If it wasn't a diet, it was some kind of exercise program. I always felt like she was ashamed of me. When I'd be successful and lose a few pounds, she'd have me come to the parlor and parade around her friends and show off. But when the weight came back on, she'd tell me to stay in my room if we had guests. Finally Grandfather found out what she was doing, and he forbade her to ever put me on another diet, or make me do exercises that I didn't want to do. After that, she paid little attention at all to me, so I spent my time alone, or with Grandfather."

"Hanna, you're a beautiful woman. Don't let Will and your mother continue to bring down your self-esteem."

"Really, Matt, you married me to save my inheritance. Your responsibilities don't include pumping up my self-esteem. But thanks, anyway."

Hanna saw anger flash in Matt's eyes.

"Is that what you think I'm doing, Hanna? I wouldn't lie to you just to make you feel better. I'm not that kind of man. I meant it when I said you're beautiful." He had moved so close, Hanna could feel the heat emanating off his skin.

Was she dreaming, or was her teenage idol, Matt Corbett, standing here, almost touching her, telling her she was beautiful? She had to be dreaming.

Her eyes left his and took in his olive complexion, the dark hair with just the faint beginning of gray in the temples, and came back to rest on his lips in time to watch them lower to cover hers.

Heat spread through Hanna's body as Matt's lips claimed hers in a tender, exploring kiss. Her knees suddenly turned to mush, but Matt's arms came around her and pulled her close, giving her support.

She felt her arms slide around his neck, and as if of their own accord her hands buried deeply into his dark hair, pulling him closer to her. His lips had turned from exploring to demanding, and Hanna parted her own to allow him to ease his tongue inside her mouth, exploring, exciting her as she had never been before.

She felt his hand work its way up her ribcage to capture a breast. Gasping with pleasure, Hanna twisted her body to allow him easier access to what he was seeking. He gently stroked her nipple with his thumb, and Hanna heard a moan escape her throat.

Slowly becoming aware of Matt's arousal pressing against her, Hanna fought her way through the fog of passion and tried to pull away.

"Matt, stop! We have to stop!" Was that squeaky voice hers?

"Why?" Matt's voice was husky. "Why do I have to stop something so wonderful?"

"Because I'm acting like a sex-starved maniac!" Hanna declared, straightening her clothes.

"I rather like how you were acting," Matt said, grinning. "I want to explore those cravings of yours." He reached for her again.

"No! Look what you've done! You've made me desecrate Grandfather's special place! Now I can't come here anymore without thinking about what I've done! I knew I shouldn't bring you up here." She sank down on a bench and buried her face in her hands.

"Hanna, what the hell are you talking about? All we did was kiss." Matt's reasoning voice came through to her.

"Maybe it was only a kiss to you, but I acted terrible! I was practically throwing myself all over you." Now her voice was stronger as she added, "I hope you don't get the wrong idea about this, Matt. This doesn't mean that we can be a real husband and wife. And it doesn't mean that I'm desperate for someone to paw over me."

"Hanna, get a grip. It was just—a—kiss. Nothing more. I'm not going to sneak into your room at night and try to claim my dues as a husband." Matt's voice held a tinge of impatience at Hanna's overreacting.

Slowly, Hanna raised her head. What a fool she was making of herself. Of course it was just a kiss. Matt was just trying to make her feel better about herself, and she had thrown herself all over him. But it meant nothing to him. As he said, it was just a kiss.

"You're right. I'm acting like a silly schoolgirl with a crush. I'm sorry. But we'd better go back to the house." She stood and led the way quickly back through the garden.

Just before they reached the house, Matt stopped her with a hand on her arm.

"Hanna, I won't go back to the gazebo unless you invite me. I won't intrude on your special spot. But I don't apologize for kissing you. In fact," he added, with a teasing smile, "I plan to make a habit of kissing you."

And he turned and left her standing alone, with only the sound of her pounding heart.

Back in the guest suite he had been allotted, Matt threw himself across the bed and stared at the ceiling. Wow! What a live wire! He could tell by the kiss he'd just shared with Hanna that she was more woman than he had ever encountered.

But he was really going to have to be careful she didn't get the impression that all he was after was sex. He had to reach her intellect. Had to find out the things she was interested in.

But every time he was around her all he could think of was how soft and desirable she looked. He felt his arousal start again, just remembering her response to their kiss.

Sitting up, he reached for the phone and dialed a number.

"Dave? This is Matt Corbett. Did you hear anything about that deal we were discussing?"

"Yeah, Matt. Can you be in the studio tomorrow around noon? Some of the boys will be in and we want to run through those lyrics you gave me."

"Great! And thanks, Dave. I owe you."

"Man, if this thing goes through, I'm the one who'll owe you. And, Matt, I meant to tell you, you're welcome to use my bike until you get a car, if you need it."

"Thanks, Dave. I believe I'll take you up on that. I hate to ask to borrow a car, here, and nobody's offered me one. Hell, I don't know if they have anything except the limo."

"You poor thing," Dave chided. "I really feel sorry for you. You're the only person I know who could lose everything he owns one week and the next week end up married to one of the wealthiest women in the country."

"Well, contrary to what you want to believe, all this wedding did for me was keep me off the streets. It hasn't put any money in my pockets, and I don't expect it to. Actually, I expect to get served with divorce papers at any minute."

Hanna stood beside the limo and watched Henri spit-shine the last spot on the long black car. She'd asked him to drive her downtown to see Houston Couch about the will. She considered taking her Jag, but she hated trying to find parking in downtown Nashville when she had a business appointment.

She loved to go into Nashville, though. Nashville had become such a mixture of the old and the new. Once she remembered exploring Nashboro Village, a replica of Nashville's first settlement. She had looked up and to her surprise realized she was seeing three generations of architecture in her line of vision.

She'd had her camera with her and took a picture capturing the logs of Old Nashboro, the old brick of the 19th-century buildings across the street, and, towering above them, the new BellSouth building everyone called the Batman Building because the twin peaks of its roofline evoked the helmet of the Caped Crusader. She thought that picture depicted Nashville to a T.

She hadn't seen Matt in two days. Not since that ill-fated trip to the gazebo. She didn't mind because she knew seeing him again would only cause her great embarrassment. She couldn't believe she'd allowed herself to act like a sex-starved woman with him.

She was beginning to regret marrying him. It would have been better to marry a real loser that she couldn't stand. That way it wouldn't be a problem to ignore him until time for the divorce.

That's why she was seeing her lawyer today. Maybe Houston could find a loophole in the will, so she could get out of this marriage before she made a complete fool of herself. Many more encounters like the gazebo, and the marriage would be consummated.

But why was Matt acting like he was attracted to her? She was sure he'd had many women in the past. After all, he'd been a big rock star. So why would he possibly be attracted to her? Did he feel obligated to act like he cared, just because he married her?

It just didn't make any sense. Unless—No. She wouldn't even let that thought come into her mind. *Unless*, her subconscious persisted, *unless he's like Mother and Will and wants to act like the marriage is real just so he can get in on the inheritance!*

"That's stupid!" She said loudly, trying to mentally shake off the unwanted thought.

"Pardon?" Henri looked up, thinking she was talking to him. "I really am trying to hurry, but you said you wouldn't be ready until nine o'clock."

"It's okay, Henri. I was just talking to myself," she assured him.

She heard the roar of the engine several seconds before the big Harley-Davidson motorcycle came into view around the curve of the driveway.

The driver slowed to a stop behind the limo and proceeded to remove his helmet. Hanna couldn't believe her eyes when she saw Matt straddling the motorcycle as if it were some wild steed.

He grinned at her open-mouthed stare and said, "Good morning, Mrs. Corbett. Like my new wheels?"

Her mind reeled. He had on a black leather jacket, and his black jeans fit so snugly she wondered how they kept from ripping as he straddled the big black bike. His hair was mussed from the helmet, and his eyes were glittering golden flecks. He looked for all the world like he belonged on a motorcycle.

And he had called her Mrs. Corbett, as if he were proud of the fact that she was. Was this part of the act? She felt as if her head would explode if she had any more unanswered questions.

Henri was scowling at Matt, daring him to stir up one single grain of dust that might mar his freshly cleaned limo, but Matt didn't seem to notice.

"Henri, is there somewhere I can park this hawg? I know you don't want it out here messing up the view."

"Just put it in the garage wherever you can find a place," Henri directed. "Are you ready Miss—Mrs. Hanna?" Henri was having a hard time remembering she was married.

"Where're you going?" Matt asked, as if he had every right to know.

"I have an appointment at the lawyer's office," she said.

"Want me to take you on this?" Again Matt was grinning, almost daring her to say yes. There was a new gleam in his eyes that she hadn't seen before. Did he get that excited about riding a motorcycle? And where did he get the money to buy a motorcycle? All his holdings had been confiscated by the IRS.

"I'll take a rain check," she promised, and heard Henri's sound of distaste.

"I'm going to remind you of that. Have you ever ridden a motorcycle?" Before Hanna could answer, he continued, "Baby, you haven't lived until you've ridden a bike. I can't wait to be the first one that you do it with."

Hanna's face was bright red as she sat quickly in the back of the limo, and Henri closed the door. Matt's words and teasing look seemed to carry a double meaning. Surely he couldn't know—

Chapter 4

"Hanna, there is no loophole. I'm sorry. I can't tamper with your grandfather's will.

"His stipulations were, you don't get the remainder of the inheritance until you have a child or until you're thirty-five. Whichever comes first. But you have to remain married to qualify for either. I'm sorry to hear that you and Matt aren't the perfect loving couple. The way he was looking at you on your wedding day sure looked like he was smitten with you."

"Houston, you can't be serious! That was the first day we'd seen each other, you know that."

"Maybe so, but maybe you should give him a chance. He might just be that special man you've waited for."

"Yeah, and he might just be after Grandfather's inheritance like a lot of other people." A touch of bitterness crept into her voice.

"Now, Hanna, don't go getting paranoid on me. That isn't like you. Go home. Relax for a while. Give this thing a chance to settle down. You might be surprised at the outcome." Houston leaned back in his leather chair and laced his fingers behind his head, giving Hanna a knowing smile.

"You're my lawyer, Houston, not my psychic, but thanks for nothing, anyway." She picked up her purse to leave.

"I'm really sorry, Hanna. I'll do a little more checking on this, but I think our hands are tied."

Hanna came slowly awake. Two weeks had passed since her meeting with Houston Couch. Two weeks she had spent trying to figure a way out of the marriage.

If she'd had any way of knowing the conditions of the will, she would never have gone through with the marriage, no matter how much her mother and Will badgered her. She admitted she could understand some of her grandfather's reasoning for leaving the will as he had, but she sure wished he'd been a little more lenient with the time factor.

She hadn't seen Matt but once in the past two weeks. He was gone when she got up, and he didn't get home until late at night, well after she had gone to bed. Sometimes she woke up to hear his shower running, and it was always past midnight.

What was he doing when he was gone? Was he seeing another woman? What if he was married to someone else? The thought crashed through her like a bolt of lightning, leaving all her nerve endings tingling. Had anyone done a background check on him? She hadn't even thought of it until just this minute.

Leaping from her bed, she checked the clock, then reached for the phone and dialed Houston Couch's phone number. Just as the recorder came on, Hanna remembered it was Saturday and no one would be in the office. Resigned to have to wait until Monday for her answer, she slipped into her silk robe and headed for the dining room.

As she drew even with Matt's door, she became aware of faint music coming from within the room. Stopping, she listened and realized Matt was singing and strumming a guitar. Engulfed with curiosity, she moved closer to the door so she could hear better.

She couldn't make out the words, but the sound of his crooning voice transported her back to the years when she'd almost worshipped him. She leaned closer to the door, trying to hear which song he was singing. She didn't recognize it as any she had on tape, and she knew she had everything he'd ever recorded.

Her eyes were closed in rapt concentration, so she didn't see or hear the approaching figure until he spoke.

"And how often do you do this, ma'am?" The voice was low and teasing.

If he hadn't stepped back, she would have knocked the coffee and Danish from his hands when she jumped.

"Don't do that!" She yelped, leaning against the wall, faint from being so startled.

"Well, how am I supposed to get into my room?" Matt asked, still amused at catching Hanna trying to hear through his door.

"You sneaked up on me on purpose," Hanna accused. "I'm sure you saw me when you came down the hallway. You could have made some kind of noise to let me know you were coming." Embarrassment had turned to anger, and Hanna's face had gone from white to crimson.

"Look, I should be the one offended. It's my door you're eaves-dropping at. What were you trying to hear?" The amusement never left his eyes, but Hanna thought she detected a slight tightening of his jaw muscles.

"You're right. I'm sorry. I heard music coming from your room, and I thought you were playing your guitar and singing. I was just trying to recognize the song," Hanna explained, feeling her anger start to subside.

"You know my songs?" Matt seemed surprised.

The chuckle was low in Hanna's throat. "Yeah. I used to listen to your stuff a little."

She didn't dare let him know her closet was full of every tape he'd ever made, duplicated by the ones that had been remade as CD's. She didn't dare let him know about the life-size poster standing just inside her closet door, and that she looked at it each night before she went to bed.

Knowing she should leave, but not wanting to, Hanna lingered against the wall.

"Why are you eating in your room?" she quizzed, noticing the balancing act he was doing, trying to hold the coffee and Danish in one hand while trying to open the door with the other.

"The atmosphere is better in my room," he said, finally turning the doorknob without any help from her. "And besides, I'm wor—I have some things I need to do."

"Oh." Hanna knew she was getting a brush off, so she turned and walked down the hall.

"Want to ride my bike today?" His voice stopped her.

"No, not today," Hanna answered, without turning, and continued down the hall.

"Scared?" he taunted, causing her to turn back to him.

He leaned casually against the doorjamb and sipped his coffee. Cut-off jeans exposed the dark hair on his legs. Legs that were strong and muscular. Hanna wondered how it would feel to have those legs entwined with her soft, smooth ones. The sleeves had been torn out of his T-shirt, and the muscles in his upper arm rippled each time he lifted the coffee cup to his lips.

Naked attraction coursed through Hanna, causing her knees to feel as if they would buckle under her. Yes, she admitted to herself. She was scared, but not of the motorcycle.

"Well, are you?" he persisted. "Poor little rich girl. Never had any fun. Never took any chances. Scared of her own shadow," he taunted.

"What time?" Hanna would show him what this poor little rich girl could do.

"Two o'clock," Matt said, looking victorious. Toasting her with his cup, he closed the door before she could change her mind.

Back in his room, Matt snapped off the tape player. Damn. That had been close. He didn't want her to hear the song until he had it finished. He was writing it about her, but wanted it to be a surprise the first time she heard it. If things went as he hoped, the song would be the first single off his next album.

He was putting in long hours in the studio, trying hard to get all the songs written for the album, so he hadn't seen much of Hanna in the past couple of weeks. He was looking forward to spending time with her today.

He grinned, remembering her reaction to his baiting. Quick to respond to lovemaking and quick to get angry.

Passionate. That's the word that summed up this woman, he concluded, becoming more anxious to explore all her reactions to life.

At exactly two o'clock Hanna came down the back stairs leading to the garage from the inside of the house. She wasn't surprised to see Matt bending over the big bike, checking everything out.

He heard her footsteps and looked up to watch her approach.

Self consciousness made Hanna want to turn and run away. Her snug jeans and tight-fitting knit top seemed to shrink a size under his keen scrutiny. Once again she was back in the parlor with her mother making her parade around for the guests, waiting for signs of approval or disapproval on their faces.

The warm glow she saw leap to Matt's eyes was all the approval she needed, and suddenly Hanna felt excitement building inside her. She had belonged to a motorcycle club briefly when she was in her early twenties, and had loved it. But the club had dispersed and she hadn't ridden in several years. She'd deliberately kept this information from Matt, just so she could use it against him when the time came. She'd teach him to taunt her like she was a child.

"Ready?" he asked when she stood beside him.

"Sure," she responded, with just the right touch of hesitancy in her voice.

Matt placed a helmet on her head, and took his time buckling the chinstrap. He studied every inch of her face as he fastened the buckle. The heat from his close body was affecting her breathing, and she willed him to hurry up before she made a fool of herself. Her eyelids felt heavy, as if they would close in preparation for the kiss she so longed for.

Startled by her thoughts, her eyes flew wide open to encounter him watching her. She felt as if he had been reading her mind, but instead of kissing her, he gently brushed his thumb across her bottom lip.

"Ready to ride?" he asked, in a voice husky with emotion. Again, Hanna wondered if his words held double meaning.

At her nod, he swung his leg over the bike and waited for her to do the same. When she was settled on the seat behind him, Matt leaned over to tell her where to rest her feet, but she already had them in position.

He cranked the bike and slowly accelerated from the garage. As he pulled out onto the highway, a shot of adrenaline electrified Hanna's body at the loud roar of the big bike. She loved the wild freedom she felt on a motorcycle.

Soon they were on Interstate 40. Hanna wondered where they were going, but was determined not to ask, since Matt seemed bent on showing her how much she had missed in life. She didn't have to wait long before she recognized the exit he took and knew he was headed for Percy Priest Lake. He didn't stop until he reached the dam.

"Want to walk around on the rocks?" he asked, taking off his helmet, then reaching to unsnap hers.

Nodding in agreement, she reached to remove the helmet, but Matt was already in the process of lifting it off of her head. She raised her hands to fluff her hair, but his large hands caught her wrists and lowered her arms to her side. Then, putting a hand on each side of her head, he gently lifted her hair and held it out so the breeze could catch it and fluff it.

"I've wanted to do that ever since I saw your picture in the paper announcing your wedding. It feels as soft and smells as good as I knew it would. It's beautiful." His fingers combed gently through the matted curls.

"My picture?" Hanna asked, surprised. "You saw my picture before you married me?"

"Yes. I was having coffee at a small coffee shop and wondering why Will wanted me to agree to marry his sister sight unseen, when my eyes fell on the paper and I caught sight of this beautiful goddess. The woman in the picture took my breath away, and I was making mental plans to call her. I had in mind to see if she would have an affair with me after I was married, because at the time I thought my bride might look like Frankenstein's mother. Then I read your name, and realized the beautiful goddess in the picture was going to be my wife, and my life took on a whole new meaning. But I couldn't, for the life of me, figure out why Will didn't want me to see you. I kept wondering if there was something weird about you. Then you explained it to me. I still think your brother is a fool."

Dumbfounded that Matt had found her picture attractive—he even used the word beautiful—and that he had married her knowing what size she was, Hanna could only gaze into his eyes. Suddenly she stood on tiptoes and planted a kiss on his lips.

"Thank you," she whispered, with her lips still touching his. His hands closed around her head and pulled her closer as his lips claimed hers. Leaning in to him, Hanna opened her mouth to his exploring tongue and would have allowed the kiss to go on forever, not caring if he thought she was wanton, but a carload of teenagers passed by, honking and hooting.

Reluctantly, Matt ended the kiss, but kept his arm around her shoulder as they started down the rocky incline.

They found a secluded spot where they could watch the sailboats, and sat down on a bed of flat rocks. The gentle lapping of the waves against the bank could have lulled Hanna to sleep, under different circumstances. But not with Matt sitting this close to her, with his thigh pressed against hers, and the hair on his arm brushing her skin each time he moved, sending tiny shivers up her spine. And now finding out he had been excited to marry her, not just knowing how she looked, but *because* of how she looked, made her even more conscious of his body close to hers. Her fantasy was becoming intertwined with reality, leaving her head swimming with unresolved emotions.

"Matt, have you ever been married before?"

"No. I've had several relationships, and one of them could have been serious, but she decided she couldn't waste her life on an entertainer. But I've never married anyone. Why do you ask?"

In turning to look at him, a light breeze caught a wisp of her hair and blew it across his face. She reached up to remove it, but his voice stopped her. "Leave it. It feels good tickling my skin."

Mesmerized by his brown gaze, Hanna forgot what she was about to say.

"Why do you ask?" he repeated his question.

"Oh!" Hanna exclaimed, remembering her question. "I just wondered if—well, you know, I just wondered if maybe—" She had to look away from him, to get control of her thoughts. She couldn't think rationally when he looked into her eyes like he was doing.

"What Hanna? What do you want to know? All you have to do is ask. My life is an open book to you."

"Well—it's just that I haven't seen you in the past two weeks, and the thought struck me this morning that you may be married to someone else, and trying to live at both places."

She expected anything but the guffaw that erupted from him.

"Hanna, if you think I'm lying to you, get your lawyer to run a check on me. But I promise you I'm not married. You'll soon know where I'm going when I leave every morning, but not yet. It's a surprise."

"I shouldn't have asked. I'm sorry." Hanna felt like a fool for even bringing up the subject.

"Why should you be sorry? You have every right to ask me a question like that. I am your husband, you know. Even if it is in name only." He gently ran the back of his fingers across her cheek. "When I agreed to marry you, before I saw the picture, I was afraid I would be expected to perform my husbandly duties in every sense of the word, and that terrified me, especially if my prospective bride looked like Frankenstein. But now, I'm sorry I didn't require a prenuptial agreement that I would be allowed to be a husband in every possible way."

Hanna knew he was kidding, but the thought made her light-headed and giddy. The sun must be getting to her, because she felt herself believing everything he said to her today, and she knew she was being foolish. But she loved the way he made her feel. So beautiful and desirable. So totally a woman. She felt a boldness she had only dreamed of. A boldness that gave her strength to play along with him.

"Well, things change, you know. If you're a good boy—" Before she could finish her sentence, Matt had laid her back on the rock and was again claiming her lips with his. One arm pillowed her head against the hard rock, but his other hand was already under her T-shirt and she could feel his flat palm resting on her bare skin.

Her free hand lightly skimmed its way up Matt's arm, feeling, touching, experiencing his strength until her fingers entwined in his thick hair, pulling him closer. She could feel his hand moving up to capture a breast. When she felt his fingers slide inside her low-cut bra to capture her nipple, she felt as if her body would turn to molten lava and blend with the rocks she lay on.

Finally, Matt raised his head and gazed at her with clouded eyes. "Woman, don't make promises you don't intend to keep. What will I get if I'm a good boy? Will I get to see these?" And he leaned down and kissed each peak through her T-shirt. "Will I get to taste them? Will I get to experience this?" And he reached down and cupped her most private spot through her jeans. "And eventually, will I get it all, if I'm really good?"

"Matt," Hanna choked out.

"No, Hanna, you started this, now tell me what I'll get if I'm a good boy," he persisted. He had plucked a strand of grass and was gently circling her mouth with it, driving her crazy with desire. She knew she had to get control, or she would let him take her right here on the hard rocks.

"No, I didn't start this," she argued, "you did."

"Yes, but you gave me hope with the 'good boy' stuff."

She tried to sit up, but he threw a leg over her and pinned her down.

"Feel what you do to me, Hanna," he said, pressing his arousal into her side. "Aren't you ashamed for making me suffer like this?" His slow hip movement only accentuated what he was saying.

Shaken and breathless, Hanna knew if she didn't make a move now, she would be forever lost. She pushed Matt away from her hard enough that she had a brief moment to sit up and escape his grasp. Standing up, she amazed herself at the speed with which she bolted up the rocky incline. She could hear him scrambling after her.

"Hanna! Come back here, right now! I'm not finished with you," he bellowed.

Hanna had reached the grass at the top of the rocks when she felt Matt grasp her ankle. Laughing hard, she pulled away from him and heard him yelp in pain. Thinking it was just a trick, she stopped and turned cautiously to look back. Matt lay on his back on the grass, clutching his right wrist to his chest.

"Matt Corbett! Is this a trick, or are you really hurt?" Hanna asked, afraid to move any closer to him.

"I think I sprained my wrist. I fell on it and twisted it." If he was faking the pain she heard in his voice, he was doing a good job of it.

Moving closer, Hanna could see from his face that he was hurting. She knelt beside him and took his injured hand in hers. He groaned softly as her fingers searched for broken bones.

"I don't think it's broken. I can't feel anything that seems out of place," she tried to reassure him.

They had parked in a parking area close to one of the public restrooms, and Hanna had an idea.

"I'll be right back," she said, hurrying toward the building where the restrooms were. She hoped against hope that there was a water cooler on the premises. She located one, then ran into the restroom and was elated to find some paper hand towels. She soaked a huge clump of the towels in the cold water and ran back to Matt, who was sitting up now.

"Here, wrap your wrist in these, and maybe the cold will keep your arm from swelling so badly until we can get home."

"Well, that's the next problem. I can't drive the bike with this arm. It may not be broken, but I don't have any grip in it."

Hanna could tell the pain was letting up, so she decided to take advantage of the opportunity to get revenge on Matt for his earlier ribbing.

"Well, maybe now might be a good time for you to apologize for making fun of me earlier," she chided.

"What are you talking about?"

"This morning when you called me a poor little scared rich girl. You know, you may have been way off base with that one." She was enjoying this immensely, even though she knew he was still in pain.

"Hanna, what in the hell are you talking about?" True confusion replaced the pain on his face.

"Apologize, and I'll tell you," she persisted.

"Okay, I'm sorry that you're a poor scared little rich girl." The twinkle was coming back into his eyes.

"No, that's not what I had in mind, and you know it." Hanna stood her ground with her hands on her hips.

"Okay, I'm sorry if I offended you. Come here and I'll kiss you to prove that I'm serious."

"That's okay. I'll take your word for it. Come on, let's go home." She reached out her hand to help him get up.

After Matt was on his feet, he asked, "And how are we going to go home? I told you I can't drive, and it's at least ten miles to the house."

Hanna went to the motorcycle and got his helmet. "Lean down and let me dress you." She knew she had said the wrong thing as soon as the words had left her mouth, and Matt's grin proved her correct.

"I'd rather you undressed me," he said, leaning close to her, trying to steal a kiss.

"Is that all you think about?" Hanna asked, playfully slapping at him and dodging his kiss.

"When you're around, I'm afraid it is." The honesty in his voice forced her eyes back to his.

"Give me the key to the motorcycle," she requested, holding her hand out.

"It's in my pocket. You'll have to get it yourself if you want it."

"What do you mean?" Hanna asked, knowing very well what he meant.

The key was in his right hand pocket, and he was in too much pain to try to get it. Could she actually reach into his pocket and get the key? Especially with his jeans as tight as they were? Her insides quaked, just thinking about the intimacy of such an act. She heard the chuckle deep in his chest, and knew he was enjoying her discomfort.

"Isn't there some way you can get the key out for me?" she asked, hoping she didn't sound as desperate as she felt.

The chuckle now became a full-fledged guffaw that showed just how much Matt was enjoying the situation.

"Oh, you're just so immature! You sound like a sixth grader who can't wait to get a girl to feel in his pocket!" she scolded, stepping close to him and making a bold movement to reach into his pocket. But her hand stuck just inside the pocket and wouldn't go any further.

"You have to hold the pocket open with one hand and work your way down with the other," he gently explained in a rough voice, all the laughter gone now.

Hanna was determined not to let Matt know how much she was being affected by being this close to him. Her hands trembled as she tried to work her way into the tight jeans. Just as her hand touched the key, she felt Matt's left hand entwine the back of her hair and tilt her head up to him. Her small puffs of breath mingled with his as he lowered his lips to hers.

Suddenly, she felt the key being pushed further into her hand, and gasped, realizing her hand was filled with Matt's excitement. The gasp allowed him further access into her mouth, which he was now fully exploring.

She must end this before she made a fool of herself! Pushing with her free hand, she made a frantic effort to bring the key out of his pocket. When she succeeded, she pushed Matt away from her. She heard him moan when their lips lost contact.

"Hanna—come on, baby. What's wrong with a little kissing? What can it hurt?"

Feeling too shaken to answer him, Hanna went to the motorcycle and straddled the big bike in the driver's seat. Soon the engine started its low growl, and Hanna looked back at an astounded Matt. "You coming with me?" she found enough voice to ask. After fumbling several times, she finally snapped her helmet in place.

"Well, I'll be damned," Matt grinned. Somehow he managed to get his helmet on without her help, then took his seat behind her. He wrapped his arms tightly around her waist and buried his nose in the side of her neck.

"Hmmm, I like this," he laughed, as she put the bike in gear and headed for the interstate.

Chapter 5

Instead of heading toward Rockwell Place, Hanna took I-40 West, headed for Nashville.

"Where are you going?" Matt yelled into her ear.

"To the emergency room to have your arm X-rayed," Hanna yelled back into the wind.

"No! I'm fine. See, I can wriggle my fingers now." To prove his point, he held his hand up in front of her and wriggled his fingers in her face.

Hanna pulled over to the side of the interstate and swung off the bike.

"Let me see," she demanded, taking his hand in hers to inspect it more closely. She could tell his wrist was already swelling, and would be sore for a few days, but there didn't appear to be any broken bones.

"Well, okay, if you really think it's not broken," she finally agreed.

Matt had sat silently watching her inspect his hand and arm. He loved the emotions that played so freely on her face without her being aware of them. He knew he was going to fall helplessly in love with Hanna, and he was determined to make her love him. He just had to find the right way to go about it.

"You can take me home and put me to bed, if you think that would help, Nurse Hanna," he teased. His voice was tender. "But you might need to get in the bed with me. I think that would really make my arm feel a lot better."

"You're terrible!" Hanna scolded, and got back on the motorcycle.

As she accelerated back into the traffic, Matt wrapped his arms tightly around her waist and held on, pulling her hard against him. Hanna reveled in the warmth of his body nestled so close to hers. What was happening to her? Where were these lustful feelings coming from? It would be so easy to let Matt teach her how to really fulfill all those feelings!

Gently smiling, and lost in her fantasy, she suddenly became aware that Matt's hands had changed positions. He was reaching under her knit shirt, and had splayed his hands across her naked midriff.

"Ahhh, now this is the way to ride a motorcycle," he said, close to her ear.

"Matt!" She scolded, trying to squirm his hands away.

"Oh, you want me to go higher?" he asked, reaching up and cupping a breast.

"No! People can see you!" she yelled back at him.

"I don't care. You're my wife. I can touch you if I want to. And besides, they can't tell what I'm doing."

He took her other breast in his other hand. "It just looks like you have enormous breasts," he laughed, and gently kneaded.

Matt's hands gently kneading her breasts and the vibration of the motorcycle were causing sensations to rush over Hanna that she had never experienced before. She would surely wreck the motorcycle if this didn't stop. Pulling over in the shadows of the first overpass she came to, she stopped the bike and sat sucking in huge gasps of air.

"Matt! You have to stop that!" she demanded, again getting off the bike.

"Why?" he asked, trying to look innocent. "Don't you like it?"

"No—yes—I mean—" Confusion jumbled her words.

"Well? Do you or not?" Matt persisted, now with a wicked gleam in his eyes.

"That's not the point! The point is, you're making a public spectacle of us, right out here in the middle of the interstate." She stamped her foot to emphasize her statement.

"You still haven't answered my question," Matt persisted.

"And I'm not going to," Hanna declared, knowing she was being backed into a corner she couldn't get out of.

"Yes you are. We're not going anywhere until you tell me you liked what I was doing." He reached over and killed the engine and took the keys from the ignition.

By now the sun was starting to set, and the shadows were growing darker under the overpass. Matt turned the lights on so approaching traffic could tell they were there.

He still straddled the bike, and motioned to Hanna, who had stepped far out of his reach. "Come here," he beckoned.

But she shook her head and thrust out her chin. He was about to get a taste of her Rockwell stubborn streak.

"*Come over here, Baby, and sit down by me.*" He started crooning one of her favorite songs. "*Come over here, and I'll show you how sweet love can be.*"

Hanna heard a groan tear its way from her throat. She couldn't believe that she, Hanna Rockwell, was standing here trying to resist the advances of Matt Corbett while he sang one of the songs she used to swoon to. She knew she would lose this battle.

She slowly made her way to him and straddled the bike, facing him. It put the two of them in an extremely suggestive position.

Matt stopped singing and slowly removed his helmet, then hers, never taking his eyes from hers.

"You are the sexiest, most beautiful woman I have ever known," he whispered, as he lowered his lips to claim hers.

The kiss was deep and exploring, and Hanna knew she was headed for quicksand. She was going to fall in love with a man who would soon be out of her life. And for that reason, she gave herself totally and tenderly to the kiss.

When Matt finally ended the kiss, he was the one heaving for air. He rested his forehead against hers until his breathing became more normal.

"Maybe we should go," Hanna suggested, without moving, not really wanting to break the spell they seemed to be under.

"You still haven't answered the question that started all of this," Matt said, the teasing note coming back into his voice.

Hanna took both his hands and placed them on her breasts, her hands covering his, pressing them close to her, and gazed into eyes that were suddenly on fire.

"Yes, Matt, I like this—No, I love it, and that scares the hell out of me. I've never had feelings like this before, and it scares me. I don't know how to handle it."

The sweet honesty of her confession made Matt's throat ache, and he made a silent promise to himself and to God that he would never hurt this woman before him. He would do what ever it took to make her happy. But now wasn't the time to tell her. She wasn't ready for his full confession of love.

So, very carefully, he placed her helmet on her head, and put his on. Then he pulled her close and laid her head on his shoulder, pulled her legs up over his, and, reaching around her, cranked the motorcycle and headed for Rockwell Place. He drove slowly, savoring the intimate position they shared, never wanting to reach Rockwell Place because then they would have to go their separate ways. He longed to share Hanna's bed. But that would come. Soon, he hoped.

Hanna was paralyzed with desire as she rode with her legs wrapped around Matt and her head snuggled close against his shoulder. Her arms tightened around him, pulling him as close as she could. She'd never known anything could be this arousing. Her whole body tingled with sexual desire, and she desperately wanted to make love to Matt Corbett.

She was sorry when they reached Rockwell Place and Matt pulled the big bike slowly into the garage.

Not wanting the night to end, neither of them was in any hurry to move from their position. Slowly, Matt removed their helmets, then wrapped his arms tightly around Hanna and gently kissed her neck through her hair. His breath was hot as he found her bare skin and started placing feather kisses on her neck, working his way up her

75

chin to lips that were parted and waiting for his. Her tongue timidly touched his, causing him to moan into her mouth.

Hanna had never wanted anything more than she wanted Matt Corbett at this moment, but slowly he ended the kiss and gazed down at her through passion-clouded eyes.

When he spoke, he voice was hoarse and sounded like a stranger. "Hanna, you're driving me crazy. If you don't want to be my wife for real, we'd better call it a night."

Hanna fell across the bed in her room. What was happening to her? She was acting like a teenager. She knew she should be a lot more cautious about her feelings for Matt, but it felt so good to feel good. She was playing with fire, but she had never been this aroused before, and, if the truth be known, she didn't want to stop what was going on. She moved her hands across the chenille bedspread and giggled at the tickling sensation that ran up her arms.

Overcome with the urge to hear the song that Matt had sung to her earlier, Hanna sprang from the bed and went to the closet. Soon she came out with the *Best of Matt Corbett* CD. In seconds, his voice was crooning from her stereo as she lay back across her bed, a faint smile playing on her lips. How she loved his voice.

Weariness from her busy day settled over Hanna. She drifted into blissful sleep, and didn't hear the soft knock on her door.

As Matt knocked on Hanna's door it opened slightly, and he realized it hadn't been totally closed. That's probably why he could hear the music when he walked past. He knocked again, quietly, and pushed the door open enough to glance into the room. He could see Hanna on her bed, and realized she was asleep. He also realized the music he'd heard in the hallway was one of his songs.

He approached the bed and looked down at Hanna. She lay on her side with her hands tucked under her chin like a child. Her right thumb and forefinger loosely clasped the ring on her left hand, as if she had gone to sleep touching it. His mother's ring. He had been hesitant to give it to Hanna at first, but now he knew she was the only woman he would ever want to wear it.

Warm pleasure engulfed him, just knowing she had gone to sleep listening to his voice and touching the ring he had given her. Could she be growing to care for him? He knew she was suspicious that he had just married her for her money, and he couldn't tell her different yet, but soon she would know that her money was the least thing he wanted or needed from her. Soon.

Longing to stay and watch her sleep, but knowing he couldn't take the chance of her waking up and catching him there, he turned to leave the room. His eyes caught sight of something familiar standing just inside the partially open closet door. Glancing back at Hanna to make sure she was still asleep, he moved close to the closet and found, looking back at him, a life size poster of himself he remembered from the years he had been a rock star.

Back in his room, pleasure flooded through Matt. Surely Hanna must care a little for him to have his tapes and a poster of him in her closet. But that poster went back for at least twelve or fifteen years, so she must have been a fan.

Smiling with pleasure, and exploring all the possibilities of what this new discovery meant, Matt soon drifted into a deep sleep.

The next morning, before going down for breakfast, Hanna slipped her long silk robe over her matching nightgown. No use to dress before she went down. She was the only one in the dining room for breakfast these days. So she was surprised to find Matt standing in front of her grandmother's portrait, sipping his coffee as he viewed the painting.

"That's Grandmother Rockwell," Hanna said softly. "I don't think Grandfather ever really got over losing her." A new shyness suddenly overcame her. She had dreamed about Matt all night, and the soft memories still lingered in her eyes. And here she was in front of him with nothing on but her negligee.

"She looks like you," Matt said, turning to face Hanna, and looking appreciatively at her apparel, before continuing. "Are your actions as much like hers as your looks are?"

"According to Grandfather, I'm her clone." Hanna couldn't keep the pride from her voice.

"Then I can see how it would be impossible to get over losing her." Matt said, looking back at the portrait.

Hanna was trying to comprehend Matt's statement when her mother breezed into the room.

"Good morning, Matt. Hanna. It's good to see you both here together. There's something I need to discuss with you.

"I think I'm going to take a small vacation. I haven't left this house in years, and now that you're married and everything has started to settle down, I think I deserve to get away and pamper myself a little. I've made reservations, and I'll be leaving for Europe day after tomorrow."

"Why, Mother, I think that's great!" Hanna exclaimed. "You should have done this a long time ago."

"Well, yes. Yes, I should have," Mary agreed, with a big smile across her face.

Hanna was always surprised at how pretty her mother was when she genuinely smiled.

"Oh, and one more thing. I'll be taking Henri with me. I don't want to travel alone. One can never be too careful these days." And she breezed from the room, just as she had breezed in.

Hanna's eyes locked with Matt's, both of them remembering Houston's revelation that Henri and her mother had been lovers for years.

"Yes. Yes," Matt said speculatively, tapping his pursed lips with his forefinger. "One can never be too careful these days."

Hanna's laugh pealed out, but she cautioned Matt to be quiet. It wouldn't do for her mother to guess they knew her secret.

They had barely contained themselves when Mary came back into the room. "Has either of you seen Will? I need to tell him about my plans."

"I haven't seen him in days," Hanna said, realizing she hadn't seen Will since the morning Matt called him down in her defense.

"No," Matt answered. "I don't see much of Will these days." And he winked at Hanna, knowing they shared the same thought.

"Well, if you see him, tell him to find me. I really must talk to him." And she was gone again.

Pouring herself a cup of coffee, Hanna spoke hestitantly, without turning to face Matt. "About yesterday—I just want to—I just think you should know—I—"

Before she could say any more, she felt Matt's hands on her shoulders, turning her to face him.

"I know. I had a wonderful time, too," he said, taking her coffee cup and placing it back beside the pot before wrapping his arms around her and pulling her close.

"Matt," she tried to protest.

"Yes, Hanna?" he answered, and started feather-kissing the sides of her mouth and down her neck.

"Matt!" Hanna tried to protest again. Someone was going to walk in on them.

"Yes, Hanna," Matt answered again, covering her lips in a deep, devouring kiss.

The feel of his cool, firm lips was driving Hanna mad. Her entire body seemed to have gone limp, and she had to wrap her arms around him just to remain standing. She timidly offered her tongue for his to play with, and was again struck with the pleasure that crashed through her, shattering all her intentions of telling Matt they needed to cool it.

She felt him tug at the sash at her waist only moments before his hands slipped inside the robe. The plunging neckline of the gown made it easy for Matt to slip his hand inside and capture a bare breast. Her gasp at his touch gave him further access into her mouth with his exploring tongue, as his thumb started working its magic on her peak.

"Oh my word!" the shocked voice exclaimed.

Jumping back as if they both had been caught in a criminal act, Matt and Hanna whirled to stare guiltily at Mary Rockwell.

"Mother! We thought you were gone." Hanna couldn't believe how dazed her voice sounded. Neither could believe the big smile that spread across her mother's face.

"I laid my sunglasses on the table, right here, and forgot them. Sorry—you kids carry on." She waved good-bye as she left the room with the big grin still on her face.

Hanna had hurriedly tied her sash back around her waist. She sat down at the long dining room table, knees too weak to hold her up.

Matt brought her coffee to her, and sat down beside her.

"You're beautiful, you know that?" His eyes were a warm glow as he held her gaze.

Hanna's throat still ached from the passion they had just shared. "You almost make me believe it," she whispered.

"You *will* believe it before I'm finished." Matt's words were a promise.

"Mr. Corbett, you have a phone call," the housekeeper spoke from the doorway.

"Thanks, I'll take it in my room," Matt answered. He leaned over and kissed Hanna softly on the lips before he left the room.

Too full of confused emotions to eat her morning bagel, Hanna sat for a long time and sipped her coffee, trying to sort out what was happening with her and Matt. But not coming up with any answers, and realizing her coffee was cold, she decided to go to her room and get dressed.

She was passing Matt's partially closed door when she heard him say, "Oh, I'll get the money from her. I've about got her convinced. I can tell she's getting ready to give in."

Too shocked to think, Hanna ran to her room. So it *was* the money he was after!

How stupid of her to even believe someone like Matt Corbett could actually be interested in her. What a fool she was. What a fool she had made of herself. And how much further would she have been willing to go, if she hadn't heard that conversation?

She had to get out of the house. She quickly showered, threw on some slacks and a loose-fitting top, and headed for the gazebo. She always went to the gazebo when she was troubled and needed to work things out.

She sank down on the bench that faced the little waterfall and, leaning her head against a post, closed her eyes. What was she going to do? She was hopelessly in love with Matt Corbett, her husband, who was only playing games with her to get her money.

She never knew that there was actual pain that came with heartache, but she was so hurt to find out the truth about Matt that her chest actually ached.

Why did she keep making herself miserable for other people? She'd married Matt to save the house and estate for Will and her mother. Now her mother was off to Europe with her lover, Henri, as happy as a lark, and Will? Well, Will was somewhere doing whatever he pleased, that was for sure. And Matt. Matt had gotten what he wanted. He'd saved his hide from the IRS. But now, it seemed he wanted more. He wanted money from her. It seemed she, Hanna, was the only one still miserable here.

"Well, that's about to come to an end," she stated aloud, startling a little bird that had landed on the step of the gazebo near her.

With a sudden clarity, Hanna made up her mind to turn her life around. She would do a few things that she had always wanted to do.

"*Which are?*" The thought came softly. Hanna thought for a moment, then answered herself aloud. "Which are, sell this house, for one thing. I'll travel abroad, and maybe even live abroad. I'll be footloose and fancy free, to do whatever I want to do. And go when and wherever I want to go. I may even take on a host of lovers to purge Matt Corbett from my soul forever."

Hoping the new plans would make her feel better, Hanna was disappointed when she realized the dead weight was still resting in the pit of her stomach as she walked slowly back to the house.

Chapter 6

"Are you sure you want to do this, Hanna?" Houston Couch had a worried look on his usually composed face.

"Yes. I'm tired of being used. I'm tired of living my life for other people who don't even appreciate what I'm doing. I want to sell the house. Surely there's no clause in Grandfather's will that says I can't sell the house, is there?" The thought brought sudden fear to Hanna.

"No. The house became totally yours in the first phase of the will. You can do with it as you please. Phase three of the will deals with the monetary aspects of your inheritance. But I can't believe you really want to sell your home. You've spent your life there. All your childhood memories are wrapped around that house and land. It's your home, Hanna."

"That's just the point, Houston. Can't you understand? I've lived my entire life in one place. I never even got to travel. Dad died when I was too young to enjoy traveling. And Grandfather was only too content to sit at home and smoke his pipe and reminisce about Grandmother. He didn't want to leave the house with all its memories, and he sure wasn't going to turn over any extra money to Mother for traveling, not even for me. So all I've ever known is Rockwell Place. I just want to get away for a while. I want to be free to go and come when I want to."

"What about your mother and Will? What will they do for a home? I thought this was the whole purpose for your spontaneous wedding. To save the house so they would have a place to live. You don't have to sell your home in order to travel, Hanna. You have money."

"Houston, do you know what my mother is getting ready to do? She's getting ready, even as we speak, to go to Europe with Henri. She says she needs to get away for a while. And of course, in her words, she needs to take Henri because she might need him."

Houston came to full attention now. "That's very interesting," he admitted.

"And who knows where Will is. I haven't seen him in over two weeks. He got angry with Matt for taking up for me, and we haven't seen him since. And I told you what I heard Matt say about getting the money from me. So why should I care what happens to these people?

"Yes, Mother and Will couldn't keep still until I agreed to get married so their future would be intact, but now look at them. I'm the only one stuck with the house, and they're out running around living life to the fullest. So why should I care what happens to them? They don't give a damn about me."

"You care what happens to them, because you are a caring person. You've convinced yourself that you don't care, but I'm afraid if you make this decision to sell Rockwell Place, you're going to regret it the rest of your life," Houston argued. "And about Matt. You didn't actually hear him call your name. What if he was talking about getting the money from someone else? What if you're mistaken?"

"I'm not mistaken. I know he was talking about me. I just felt it. Houston, I am putting the house on the market, so find a Realtor."

Hanna's mind was made up.

"Did she give you the money?" Dave asked when Matt came through the door.

"Of course she did. I told you I had her eating out of the palm of my hand," Matt said with a cocky twitch of his eyebrow.

"You lucky dog. We should all have a rich aunt. Where was she when your manager got you in financial trouble? Why didn't you go to her then, instead of getting married to a stranger?"

"Dave, I guess I have too much pride to ask my mother's favorite sister for money when I'm in trouble, but this is different. This is an investment for her. If this album does good, she'll make a lot of money off the backer's percentage I'm giving her, so I don't feel bad about asking her to do this. Especially after all the good vibes we've gotten from these songs. I'm actually doing my aunt a big favor by getting her involved in my future. That is, if things go like they seem to be headed. I hope to hell I'm not going to be the cause of her losing money. But I did explain all of the ramifications of this gamble to her."

"I do believe we're on to something big, friend. I'm just glad I'm a part of this. This is going to be one of the major career comebacks of the decade. I can hardly wait to see your fans' reaction." Dave's eyes were alight with excitement.

"Do you think my fans will accept me as a country artist? They were rock fans, you know." A tinge of doubt sounded in Matt's voice.

"Hey, now, don't go get cold feet on me. Sure, they'll accept you. They're all older now, and a lot of them have probably switched to country music anyway. And besides that, this new country sound is a lot like the rock sound a few years ago. You wrote these songs, so they still sound like you, they just have a country twist. The whole world is going to love you. You're going to be the next Garth Brooks!" Dave's reassuring words restored Matt's confidence, and he grinned.

"Thanks, Dave. I'm glad I have at least one fan."

Several days later, Hanna was sitting on the deck with her morning coffee when Will burst through the sliding glass door leading from the dining room.

"Just what the hell is going on here?" he shouted, bearing down on Hanna.

Startled, Hanna almost dropped her coffee mug.

"What are you talking about, Will?" she asked innocently, knowing he must have spotted the "For Sale" sign in front of the house.

"You know damn well what I'm talking about! Who put the sign out front? And why?" Hanna had seen Will lose his temper before, but this time, he really looked out of control.

"Settle down, Will, and let's talk," she admonished. "I'm selling Rockwell Place."

"Like hell you are!" he exploded. "Over my dead body."

"What do you care? You're never here. And now that you have your allowance from Grandfather's will in place and don't have to worry about that, why do you care if I sell the house?" Hanna hoped to calm him down with her reasoning.

"You can't put this place on the market, Hanna. I'm telling you right now, you'd better call that real estate agent and tell them to come get the sign if you don't want me to use it as a bonfire right where it is. I'm not asking you, Hanna, I'm telling you."

Hanna had never felt threatened by Will before when they argued, but this time was different. His normally tanned face was chalky white, and she could see his hands trembling.

"Will, what's wrong with you? Are you threatening me? Why do you care so much about this house all of a sudden?"

"You fat, selfish bitch, you just better do as I tell you!" He reached out and slapped the coffee mug, splashing hot coffee onto the front of Hanna's body. He turned to go back into the house and walked right into Matt's fist.

Matt had been standing at the open door listening to Will's outburst. When Will slapped the coffee all over Hanna, it was the last straw.

Matt's first punch landed square on Will's nose, jarring him backward. Matt barely heard Hanna's sharp cry of surprise before his left hand landed upside Will's head, staggering him back away from Hanna. Matt's third punch took Will to his knees.

Matt was silently thankful for the barroom brawls he'd taken part in as a younger man. It gave him the practice and know-how he needed now. Before he had a chance to follow through with another punch, Will moaned and fell forward on the deck.

Shaking his bruised and already swelling hands, Matt went to Hanna and took the mug from her trembling hands.

"Are you okay?" he asked, checking to see if the coffee had burned her anywhere.

His tenderness, coming on the heels of the chaos that had just taken place, was more than Hanna could stand. Looking up at him, her chin quivering with tears that were threatening to start, all she could do was nod her head.

"Baby, don't cry," Matt said, dropping to his knees and wrapping his arms around her. But his gentle concern only caused the dam of tears to break, and Hanna couldn't hold back the hurt any longer. She sobbed into Matt's shoulder.

Neither of them heard Will struggling to his feet, and didn't know his intentions until he slammed a wrought iron patio chair across Matt's back, knocking him to the floor, groaning in pain.

"If you know what's good for you, you'll take this house off the market today," Will snarled at Hanna and stormed from the deck.

Hanna dropped to her knees. "Matt, is anything broken? Are you okay?" She reached out to touch his back, but he rolled over and made a feeble attempt to sit up.

"What in the hell is wrong with your brother?" he asked, turning one way, then the other, testing to see if he had any broken ribs.

"I don't know, but he sure is upset about me putting the house on the market."

"Why are you doing that, Hanna? I saw the sign last night when I came home." He pulled himself up into a chair and sat down, moaning slightly as he leaned back into the chair.

"You okay?" Hanna asked, watching him closely, using her concern to put off answering the question as long as possible.

"I'm okay," Matt assured her. "My back hurts like hell, but I don't think I have anything broken."

"Do you think we need to take you to the doctor?"

"Hanna, stop hedging. Why are you selling the house?"

"Why not?" she asked. "Mother's traveling now. Will's never here anymore, and you're always gone until the wee hours of the morning, so I seem to be the only one rattling around in this huge house by myself. So could someone please tell me why I need to keep the house?"

"Because it was your grandfather's, and it is your heritage, and you know you love it. I think you'll really regret it if you sell it. Maybe not now, but later on when you get older, you'll really wish you had kept it, especially when you have children. Think of the special gazebo your grandfather built for you. Don't you want to share that with your children?"

"Children? Matt, get real. I'm thirty years old, and fat. Do you really think I'm going to meet someone who will love me and make children with me before all my eggs are so old they're using a cane?"

"Hanna, I'm your legal husband. If you want a baby, we can make one right now."

Hanna stared at Matt, open-mouthed. She tried to speak, but words wouldn't come.

"I'm serious, Hanna. Let me give you a baby, so you can get the rest of your inheritance, and see the end of this nonsense. Maybe if you did have a baby, your mom and Will would give you a little peace."

"What? I can't believe you think I would stoop low enough to bring a child into this world just to help my own cause! What kind of person do you think I am? And what kind of person are you to even suggest such a thing?" Hanna couldn't believe Matt had made such a crazy suggestion.

"Wait, Hanna. Don't jump to conclusions. I thought you meant you wanted a baby, when you said you couldn't find anyone before your eggs got too old."

"So, out of pity you just volunteered to help me out? Give me a break, Matt. I don't need your pity." Hanna started toward the door back into the house.

"I know *that's* right," Matt's sarcastic voice stopped her. "You have enough self-pity of your own. You sure don't need anyone else's."

"What's that supposed to mean?" Hanna asked, dumbfounded.

"Hanna, do you ever listen to yourself? You constantly put yourself down, and by doing so, you invite other people to do the same thing. Then you get all hurt and full of self-pity. And when someone does try to compliment you, or just treat you like a normal person, you get all defensive at that. Until you start thinking of yourself as a normal, okay person, you can't expect anyone else to treat you like one." Matt knew he was saying too much, but he had waited too long to say it.

"Just when has anyone tried to build me up? Or compliment me? I don't believe I've heard any of that. Where was I?" She tried to make her voice hard, but the quiver came through anyway.

"What about me, Hanna? Haven't you heard any of the things I've said to you? I've even fought for you, and may have a broken knuckle even as we speak." He looked down at his swollen hand to make his point.

"True, but you're getting well paid for your services. Marrying me saved your skin from the IRS, gave you a place to live, and food to eat. So, I'm sure you feel obligated to say and do all the right things. It's not like you're saying them because you really mean them. And, by the way, I heard you on the phone telling someone you would get some money from me. Just figure out how much you need and let me know. I'll write you a check."

Hanna slammed the door so hard behind her she was afraid the glass was going to shatter. Her anger carried her up the stairs to her room with so much momentum that Matt heard her bedroom door slam before he could even get his mouth closed.

So that was it. She'd overheard him talking to Dave about his aunt's loan, and assumed he was talking about her. Matt didn't know whether to go to her and show her how much she turned him on, or just leave her alone and let her anger wear off.

Maybe he'd better just leave her alone for now. She sure seemed determined to sell the house all of a sudden. But where did that leave him? It was a shame. He had already grown to love this old house and surrounding estate. If he just had the money, he'd buy it—

Two days later, the real estate agent called and informed Hanna someone had put a contract on the house. They hadn't tried to negotiate, and didn't even want to take a tour of the place. They just wanted to buy it, sight unseen.

"But when do I have to be out?" Hanna asked her, feeling apprehension creep up her spine.

"Apparently, there's no hurry. She said just whenever was convenient for the owners.

"She? Did you get a name? Is it a family?" Suddenly, Hanna wanted to know who was going to live in her dear home.

"It was a strange thing," the real estate agent said. "This older lady came in and just wrote a check for the total amount. Said I could keep the check until all the paperwork was cleared, then I could let her know. She must be buying it for her children or grandchildren."

After getting off the phone, Hanna sat for a long time, staring into space. It was done! She had sold her home.

Doubt flooded her, making her eyes fill with tears. She'd expected it to take longer for Rockwell Place to sell. What was she going to do now? She hadn't had time to even come up with a plan, other than just put everything in storage and travel for a while. Well, so be it. That's what she would do.

She hadn't seen Matt since she had stormed away from him two days ago. She felt a little guilty to have been so hard on him after he'd jumped on Will like he had in her defense, but he'd asked for it by all those things he'd said to her.

Telling her to act like a normal person and the whole world would treat her normal. Yeah, right! Like it was easy as all that.

What if he's right? The question came from nowhere. If only it could be that easy, she thought with a deep sigh.

Matt. Thank goodness she'd heard his conversation about the money when she did. She'd been so captivated by his charm that she'd been about ready to jump in bed with him. What a fool thing that would have been to do.

But just thinking about the way he kissed and touched her made her whole body ache and yearn to do more than just be kissed by Matt Corbett. What a wimp she was, she scolded herself. Even knowing he was just using her to get to her money almost didn't matter when she remembered how good it felt to be in his arms.

That's why she had to get away from Rockwell Place. Away from Matt Corbett. Before she did something really stupid like going to bed with him. Or even more stupid like letting him know she was hopelessly in love with him.

Chapter 7

The impatient ringing of the doorbell interrupted Hanna's morning. Remembering that Lena, the housekeeper, had taken the morning off, Hanna hurried down the stairs to find out who could be visiting this early in the day.

Who could it be? Her mother and Henri had left for Europe yesterday, and she hadn't seen Will since his fight with Matt, well over a week ago.

Looking through the peephole in the door, she saw two men in suits standing, casually talking, so she opened the door.

"Yes?" she inquired, taking in the expensive-looking clothes the two men wore. They had an unusual look that she couldn't quite place. Almost like the men she had seen in movies that portrayed the Mafia. The thought brought a slight smile to her lips, until the tallest man spoke.

"Yeah, we're lookin' for Will Rockwell. Y'know where we can find him?"

A chill started a slow crawl up Hanna's spine. What had her brother gotten himself into this time? These men were not playing games. Their eyes were cold and hard, and their poor grammar belied the expensive suits.

Hanna tried to close the door, but the tall one, moving quickly, stuck his foot in the crack before she could get it closed.

"Oh, no you don't, lady. Not until we can find that no good bastard that made off with our money. And what's that sold sign doin' out front? This is supposed to be our collateral if he can't pay his debt." Not waiting for her answer, he pushed his way inside, the shorter one close on his heels.

"I'm Hanna Rockwell." Hanna's fear gave way to anger. "This is my house, and Will is my—"

"Morning, gentlemen." Matt's quiet voice interrupted Hanna. She glanced around to find him standing with a gun aimed at the two men.

"You boys have a seat and let's talk about this," he said. Hanna couldn't believe the controlled fury in his voice.

"Ain't nothin' to talk about," said the tall one, sitting on the couch. "Will's been real free with his gamblin', and he ain't real good at it, and he used this house for collateral in case he lost and didn't have the money to cover his debt, just like I told the lady."

"We don't know where Will is. But one thing's for sure, this house wasn't his to use as collateral. He doesn't own any part of this house," Matt told the men.

"Well, that ain't real good for poor Will. This was his last time to screw up. The Boss told him if he did it again, he wouldn't live to tell about it. I don't know what he is to you two, but you might as well kiss his ass good-bye, cause he's a goner."

"How much does he owe?" Hanna asked.

"Hanna!" Matt said in a warning voice.

"How much?" she persisted, ignoring Matt.

"Ten grand," the tall one answered.

"Promise me you won't hurt Will, and I'll have the money for you tomorrow. But I want your boss to meet with my lawyer and sign an agreement that he will never do business with Will again, and that Will's life won't be in any danger. Do we have a deal?"

"Can I use your phone to call the Boss? We had instructions not to come back without Will or the money."

"Here," Matt said, throwing him his cell phone.

Soon the two threatening men were out of the house, and the door was soundly locked.

"So that was why Will threw such a fit when he found out the house was for sale. He knew if those goons saw the sign, they'd be after him," Matt said, sinking into the nearest chair.

Hanna sat down on the couch, but couldn't seem to take her eyes off the gun still clutched in Matt's hand.

Catching the direction of her eyes, Matt quickly shoved the gun into his pants pocket.

"Don't worry about the gun, Hanna. I've been registered to carry guns since my days on stage. Can't be too careful, you know."

Suddenly, tears welled up and spilled out of Hanna's eyes and rolled down her cheeks. She tried to wipe them quickly away before Matt could notice. It seemed like she was always blubbering when he was around, and she hated for him to think she was just a silly crybaby.

97

But he saw the tears and was quickly on the couch beside her, slipping an arm around her shoulder.

"Hanna, don't," he said, taking her chin in his hand and lifting her face to his. "We'll take care of this. We'll bail Will out this time, and maybe he'll learn a lesson from this mess he's in."

Hanna gazed deeply into Matt's calming eyes. He always seemed to show up at the right time to defend her. First from Will and her mother, now from those two goons. Just like her knight in shining armor. So what if he needed money from her? He had come to her rescue even when he agreed to marry her, hadn't he? If not for him, she wouldn't have as much of her inheritance as she had. He really was her knight in shining armor, she thought, a smile playing around the corners of her lips.

Her quivering lips, trying to smile even in the face of yet another trauma, were more temptation than Matt could stand. Even though he still stung from her accusing him of wanting her money, he couldn't stop himself from lowering his lips to hers.

The rejection he expected didn't come. Instead, he felt her lips yielding under his, and returning his kiss. How he wanted to take her up to his room and consummate their marriage! Every fiber in his body wanted to make love to her and show her what a desirable woman she was, and how much she turned him on. He wanted to get lost in her womanly body, and spend time exploring all the ways that turned her on. But not yet. She wasn't ready yet.

Slowly, he ended the kiss and raised his head to gaze down into her half-closed eyes. He knew from the first that it was inevitable he would fall in love with her, but nothing could have warned him of how deep his feelings would go for her this soon. As he gazed down at her upturned face, awareness dawned on him. He was irrevocably, deeply in love with Hanna Rockwell!

Before the realization could totally sink in, the front door burst open and Will stormed into the room. But it wasn't the belligerent, cocky Will they usually encountered. He was tired and worn looking, and looked as if he hadn't had a bath in a week.

"Hanna, you have to help me. I'm in deep trouble," he pleaded, dropping to his knees in front of them. "Those two men that were just here are going to kill me if they find me. They're—" He couldn't go on from the emotion in his voice.

"I know, Will." Hanna almost felt pity for her half-brother. The brother she had always wanted to be close to. She had always wanted them to be friends, but Will had seemed to hate her so much.

"You do?" Suddenly he was all attention.

"Yes. Houston Couch is going to talk with The Boss tomorrow, but you and I have a lot of talking to do first. I'm glad you're here."

Three days later, Hanna and Matt stood at Nashville International Airport and watched an airplane lift off with Will on board. After settling all his debts, Houston Couch had decided the best thing for Will to do was to disappear and get a change of scenery for a while. He was headed for Europe to join his mother and Henri.

Without Matt knowing, Hanna had reimbursed Will for all the money he had spent on Matt's IRS debts and residence before the wedding.

"I know they're so happy that he's joining them," Hanna said with a soft chuckle, as the plane disappeared into the blue horizon.

"You have a real mean streak, don't you?" Matt teased her. Ever since the revelation that he was in love with Hanna, he couldn't keep his eyes off her. She had so much to offer a man. Somehow, he had to make her realize that.

"No! I don't have a mean streak. They deserve each other," Hanna declared, having to look away from the fire in Matt's eyes.

Was she just imagining it, or had his attitude changed since the day the goons had come by the house? He looked at her with such intensity that she was either lost in his gaze, or had to look away for fear of being engulfed in it.

As they walked though the airport terminal, Hanna watched women glance at Matt. Some, she was sure, recognized him, but some were just looking because he was so handsome. She was also acutely aware of his hand in the center of her back, guiding her and steering her through the bustling people. Occasionally he would put his arm across her shoulder and walk so close their hips brushed against each other.

They had brought Will to the airport in Hanna's Jag. Once back inside it, Matt suggested, "why don't we go out to the Opryland Hotel and walk around. When we get tired we can stop and have a drink and dinner in the Cascades restaurant and listen to the water-fall."

"That sounds great," Hanna quickly agreed, not wanting to end the day with Matt.

They strolled around the hotel's Conservatory for a couple of hours, enjoying the exotic plants and each other's company. Hanna really loved the new addition called The Delta, with its New Orleans feel. They rode in one of the riverboat rides that floated down the "river" running through the area, past retail shops, a jazz bar, and meandering walkways that wound through lush trees and flowers. It was extremely romantic to Hanna, and for a brief few moments she pretended they were a real couple, on a real honeymoon, lost in some distant land. She was sorry when the ride came to a halt.

Matt continued to be attentive, either holding Hanna's hand or resting his arm around her shoulder. She almost had the feeling he wanted the world to know she was his, but that was just one of her silly romantic thoughts. Yet it felt so good to walk with him and feel almost as if they were one. As if they were connected in that special way lovers connect.

When they walked through the tunnel under the waterfall in the Cascades, they stopped to gaze out of the little window looking out into the falling water. They were totally alone, and Matt turned Hanna's face up to him and softly kissed her parted lips. It was a long, exploring kiss, and would have gone on longer if they hadn't heard a tiny snicker and looked around to find two little girls watching them.

"Are you married?" one asked, openly staring at Matt.

"Yes we are," Matt answered, smiling at the little girl. "Then you can keep on kissing her," the little girl said, and the two skipped off, holding hands.

"Okay, I will," Matt whispered, and again lowered his lips to Hanna's.

Emotion flooded Hanna as she stood under the covered bridge, water cascading nearby as Matt's lips claimed hers. She turned fully to him and slipped her arms around him. He pulled her tightly against him.

Overcome with the romance of the evening, and feeling her love for him well up inside her, Hanna gave herself totally to Matt's kiss. She held back nothing as she returned his kiss deeply, giving her heart and soul to the only man she had ever wanted.

Matt, sensing a change in the way Hanna was responding to him, felt his arousal start. He had to get control, or he would embarrass himself right here in public. He pulled away from her reluctantly.

"You're driving me crazy, Hanna. Can't you see how much I want you?" His breath was coming in short puffs, ragged with emotion.

To Hanna, lost in her feelings of love for him, his declaration of desire was almost as good as a declaration of love.

"I guess we'd better go get dinner," Matt whispered into her ear.

"Or we could just go home," Hanna whispered back, brushing her lips softly against his as she talked.

"What are you saying?" Matt demanded, suddenly alert.

"Whatever you want me to be saying," Hanna answered, kissing one corner of his mouth, then the other.

"Come on, woman. Let's get out of here before I make a fool of myself."

In the car, speeding towards Rockwell Place, Hanna questioned the sanity of what she was about to do. But why not? He was her husband. He hadn't said he loved her, but he did say he wanted her. Wanted *her*. Her—Hanna Rockwell. And she could tell from the reaction of his body that he wasn't just making it up. And she loved him. She had always done the correct thing. Miss Do The Right Thing was who she had always been.

Well, tonight she was going to do what she *wanted* to do, whether it was the right thing or not. What could be wrong with making love with your husband, especially if you were in love with him?

"Hanna, are you sure about this?" Matt asked, locking the door behind them as they entered Rockwell Place.

"I'm sure, Matt. Are you?" Hanna wondered if he was having second thoughts. How embarrassing if he said he didn't want her now.

"Feel how sure I am," he answered, placing her hand on his hardness. "But I don't want you to do something you'll regret tomorrow. I want you to wait one hour and think about what you're doing. I'll be in my room, if you want to continue." He left her standing there, staring at his departing back as he headed up the stairs.

Hanna watched him go, loving him more because he hadn't taken advantage of her in a vulnerable moment. She went to her room and headed for the bathroom. She ran steaming water into the tub and took a long, leisurely bubble bath, letting the rose scent sink into her flushed skin.

When she had finished her bath, she went to her closet and took out a beautiful white negligee and slipped it on. It enhanced her large breasts, and Hanna smiled at her image in the mirror. Her mother had bought the negligee for her first night on her honeymoon. Well, tonight wasn't a honeymoon, but it was probably the closest thing she would ever come to having one. Tonight she felt beautiful. It was a totally foreign feeling to her, but she loved the way it felt. How she wished she could feel like this always. But if not, then tonight would be enough. She practically floated down the hall to Matt's door.

Matt lay on his bed, chiding himself for being such a fool. "Take an hour and think about it?" He must have sounded like a complete nerd. Hanna had probably gone to her room, had a good laugh and was already asleep.

103

He had to go to her. He had to let her know he wanted her with all his being. He didn't know if he was ready to confess his love yet, but he had to make love to her tonight.

As he reached for the doorknob, he heard the soft knock. He opened the door to find an angel in white, smiling hesitantly at him.

"You came," he whispered, drawing her to him.

"Of course I did," she whispered back, wondering how he could have doubted she would.

Taking her hand, Matt led Hanna to his bed and gently lowered her onto it. The only light in the room was a lamp on the night table, just enough to cast a romantic hue over the bed.

Hanna watched as Matt slowly unbuttoned his shirt and let it slide to the floor. His chest was covered with a layer of tiny dark curls a shade darker than the hair on his head. She felt excitement charge through her as she visually traced the hair until it disappeared in a peak at the top of the beltless slacks resting loosely around his hips.

She watched, mesmerized, as he placed a knee on the bed beside her and lowered himself down to her, devouring her body with his eyes.

"I'm going to make love to you all night. Over and over and over. I'm going to kiss every inch of your body. And when I'm finished, you're never again going to doubt that you're beautiful. And you're going to know that you're worthy of any man's love."

And he proceeded to do all he had promised.

Hanna awoke slowly the next morning, awareness of the sun shining in her face coming at the same time as the realization that she wasn't in her own bed. Then she became aware of Matt, lying beside her, propped up on one elbow, watching her.

"Good morning, Sleeping Beauty," he greeted her.

"Good morning," she returned shyly, remembering the phenomenal night she had just spent. Matt had awakened fires inside her that she never knew existed. And just as he had promised, she did feel beautiful. So beautiful that she loved having him look at her the way he was doing, almost as if he loved her as much as she loved him.

She was so glad she had followed her impulse and spent the night making love with him. He had slowly loved away all the old self-doubt and inhibitions that her mother and Will had instilled in her all these years. They would never be able to hurt her any more.

"Why didn't you tell me?" he asked, tracing her lips with his finger.

"I was embarrassed," she answered, knowing what he meant without asking.

"Why would you be embarrassed about being a virgin?" Real sincerity sounded in his voice.

"An old one, don't you think? Most women don't make it to my age with that claim to fame. Or maybe I should say claim to shame."

"There's no shame in waiting until you find the person you want to place that honor on. And I do feel honored. No matter what happens to us in the future, I'll always treasure the night we just spent. But I am worried about one thing. Are you on any kind of birth control?"

"Oh—my—goodness!" Hanna exclaimed, sitting straight up in bed. The thought had not crossed her passion-fogged mind last night. And apparently, it hadn't crossed Matt's, either.

"Can I take that as a no?" Matt asked, deep concern in his voice.

"Oh, what have I done? What if I'm pregnant?" Hanna wailed, falling back onto her pillow, forgetting that she was totally nude.

"Well, one thing's for sure, a baby will have plenty to eat," Matt said with a husky voice, as he cupped one of her breasts in his hand, and leaned over to take the peak in his mouth.

Suddenly, the fear of being pregnant was lost to Hanna as the beautiful sensation Matt was causing overtook her. So what if she *was* pregnant ? That was what Grandfather had wanted, anyway. It would just speed up the finalization of the will. And at this point, with Matt arousing her like he was doing, she would gladly give him half of everything she had if he would just promise to make her feel this way forever.

Later, as they lay exhausted and satiated with love, but having taken proper precaution against getting pregnant, the shrill ringing of Matt's cell phone startled them both.

"Hello?" Matt spoke into the phone.

After listening for a long time to the caller, Matt jumped from the bed in apparent jubilation. "Really, man? Really? Man, you wouldn't shit me, would you? Damn! That's fantastic! Sure! I'll be down there as soon as I can get dressed!"

After hanging up the phone, Matt turned to Hanna. "Baby, I hate like hell to do this, but I really have to go take care of some business. I can't tell you what's going on, yet, but I will as soon as I can. You do trust me, don't you?"

"Sure," mumbled a puzzled Hanna. But her reply was lost on Matt, who had already disappeared into his bathroom and started the shower running.

"Well, I guess that's that," Hanna thought dejectedly, as she gathered her negligee and headed for her room.

She was searching in her closet for something to wear when she felt Matt's arms come around her from behind, and felt his mouth nuzzle the back of her neck.

"Baby, don't leave me like that. I came back from my shower and you were gone. Don't be mad at me because I can't tell you what I'm doing. It's going to be a really great surprise for you, I promise. Okay?"

Frozen in place, Hanna murmured, "Okay." She had to get him out of her closet before he discovered the poster of himself standing just inside the closet door.

"Oh, and just for a clue, maybe you'll soon have a new one of these," he said, indicating the poster she was so afraid he would spot. Then he was gone, leaving her more puzzled than ever. He hadn't seemed at all surprised at seeing a poster of himself in her closet, and what on earth did he mean by "having a new one"?

Hanna took a slow shower and relived the night before. She couldn't keep the smile off her face. All her life she had dreamed of a night like last night, but never thought she would actually experience it. Matt had fulfilled his promise to make love to her all night. He had made a slow, easy love to her that nearly drove her crazy with wanting him.

Would this be the only night they would spend together? Not if she had her way. She put the thought of being pregnant far from her mind. If it happened, she'd deal with it when she had to.

She floated through the day in a haze of happiness. All her life she'd imagined that this was the way marriage should be, but she never, in her wildest dreams, expected to experience this kind of bliss. The sun was brighter. The flowers smelled sweeter. And everything she did had an added intensity.

That night, Hanna took a long, leisurely bubble bath and put on one of her sexiest negligees. She brushed her hair and put on the lightest touch of makeup and a dab of perfume, then waited in her room until the wee hours of the morning, but Matt never came home. Finally, exhausted, she fell asleep on a pillow that was damp with her tears.

Across town, Matt glanced at his watch. Damn! Hanna was going to think he was such a jerk. But he couldn't call from the studio. They were laying down the track on the last song for the album, and he needed to stay and hear what was going on.

When Dave had called this morning, saying the deal was closed and a major label had agreed to produce Matt, he had wanted to tell Hanna with all his heart—but he also wanted to wait until the whole thing was complete, so he could surprise her and at the same time let her know he didn't need her money, but he wanted *her*. More than anything in the world, he realized now, after spending the night making love with her. And he knew he was ready to declare his love. But he wanted to wait on that, too, until he could do it as an independent man. So she would know he wanted her for who she was and not for her money.

Chapter 8

The sounds of the busy bank surrounded Hanna as she sat and waited to see the president, Sam Coolly. Sam had been friends with her grandfather for as long as she could remember, and even though she knew any of the vice presidents could be with her when she opened her grandfather's lockbox, she wanted Sam to be there. Someone who had known Grandfather, and would understand her reactions, whatever they would be, when she saw the contents that Grandfather had referred to in his video.

When she woke up that morning and Matt still wasn't home, she was more determined than ever to get on with her life. She'd been trying to find time to check out the lockbox, and this morning seemed to be the time.

She had tried to busy herself all morning and not think about Matt and the lonely night she had spent waiting for him to come home, but that was all she could think about.

Her life was changed forever, and she had no regrets. But why would Matt say all those wonderful things to her, and make love to her like she had never dreamed love could be made, and then leave and not come home and not even call to say he wouldn't be home for the night? Had their night of lovemaking meant nothing to him?

She felt the old self-doubt trying to rear its ugly head, but she quickly fought it down. She was through with those negative thoughts about herself, no matter what the future with Matt held.

"Hello, Hanna." Sam's kindly voice interrupted her reverie. "Come on into my office. I've sent someone after the lockbox."

A young executive bustled into Sam's office seconds after Hanna had been seated. Sam handed her a key, and with much trepidation Hanna slowly opened the lid to the box.

The first item her eyes fell upon was a note scribbled in her grandfather's handwriting. *"The contents of this lockbox are the sole property of Hanna Rockwell. No one else is to see the contents."* She found an envelope with her father's wedding band in it, and one with her grandmother's wedding ring set. There were several pictures of her grandparents when they were newlyweds, and some when her father was a baby. Finally, at the bottom of the box was a brown manila envelope with no title on it.

Knowing this envelope must hold the information her grandfather had referred to, Hanna's hands trembled as she took it from the box and started to open it. It was sealed, then taped, as if to assure that it didn't come open on its own. Taking the letter opener Sam offered, Hanna gently slit the top of the envelope and pulled out a folder.

She closed her eyes briefly, then glanced at Sam for support. When she opened the folder, another note from Grandfather lay on top.

"Hanna, examine the contents of this envelope very carefully. Then proceed as you see fit. You will find a marriage license that shows your mother secretly married Henri two weeks after your father died. I wanted to throw her out of my house at that time, but I knew she would try to take you, and I couldn't do that to you or myself, as I wanted to watch over you as you grew up. You will also find the blood test proving Will is Henri's son.

"The contents of this envelope prove without a shadow of a doubt that you are my sole heir, and that your mother and Will are entitled to nothing unless you wish to deem it so.

"Documentation of these facts is also in the possession of Houston Couch and his firm, in case you run in to any legalities with your decisions.

"As always, I hope you know how much I have loved you.

Grandfather."

Tears flowed freely down Hanna's cheeks as she finished reading the note.

After taking a few moments to gain control, Hanna looked up into the concerned eyes of the old banker.

"Do you know what these documents say?" Hanna asked him.

"Yes. Your grandfather made sure I knew what this box held, and that I knew how important it was to your future. Would you like copies of the documents?"

"Yes," Hanna answered, not knowing why, but feeling sure she would have to use them soon.

Hanna left the bank with copies of the facts that could change her mother's and Will's lives forever, if she so wished.

She felt lonelier than she had ever felt in her life. Knowing that her mother loved Henri enough to marry him and risk losing her share of the Rockwell estate if the truth were ever found out, made Hanna understand why her mother had always treated her the way she had. She had never wanted her, because she was the child of the man she didn't love. Will, on the other hand, had been conceived in love, and that's why her mother had always been partial to him.

And now Grandfather, the only person in the world who had ever loved her, was gone.

And she had foolishly fallen in love with her husband. And he, obviously, only wanted her for her money.

Lost in self-pity, Hanna didn't hear the low idle of the motorcycle until a familiar voice said, "Hey, Beautiful, going my way?"

Startled, she looked up to find Matt walking his bike along the curb beside her.

Gladness at seeing him caused her heart to leap into her throat—until she remembered she was supposed to be angry with him.

"Go to hell," she said, turning quickly into the underground parking garage where her car waited.

Hanna could tell by the increasing roar of the motorcycle that Matt was following her. She hurried to her car to try to get in before he caught her, and had her hand on the door handle, opening it, when his large hand covered hers.

"Baby, don't be mad at me. I wanted to call you, but you've just got to believe me when I say I couldn't. I was just on my way home to try to explain to you."

The sincerity in his voice almost made Hanna believe him. His closeness caused a tremor to pass through her, remembering their night of lovemaking. How she wanted to go into his arms and forgive him, and believe whatever lies he might tell her.

"I'll see you at home," Hanna said, trying to keep her voice cold, but feeling herself weaken. She had to get away from him before she fell into his arms and begged him to take her right here in the parking garage.

Matt gave in and opened the door for her. But before he closed it, he leaned down and quickly kissed her.

Driving toward Rockwell Place, with Matt following close behind on his bike, Hanna felt her previous tension and self-pity draining from her. How could she stay angry with Matt when she loved him so much? She would be back in his bed tonight if he asked. She felt her insides start to melt just thinking about it.

The door had barely closed behind them when Matt reached for her and captured her lips in a hungry kiss that took her breath away.

"I couldn't wait to get back to you," he whispered against her hair.

"Well, that didn't appear to be the case," Hanna said, pulling slightly away from him, remembering the hurt of waiting up almost all night for him.

"Did you wait for me?" Matt asked, hoping she had, yet feeling horrible about not being able to call her.

"Until three o'clock," Hanna answered, scolding him with her eyes.

"Baby, I'll make it up to you," Matt promised, taking her lips in his again.

"How?" Hanna asked, wanting more than anything to feel like a total woman in his arms again.

"First, I'm going to kiss you here," Matt said, gently touching each breast. "Then I'm going to kiss you here," he said, slowly running his hand down her hip and cupping between her legs. "Then I'm going to touch you and hold you and love you until you forgive me for making you wait for me."

Hanna dropped her purse and the envelope on the hall table, and let Matt lead her upstairs to his room.

Holding her hand as if afraid she would try to escape, he went around to each window and opened the curtains wide to let the bright sunlight flood the room. Then he turned to Hanna and started slowly undressing her.

"I want to see you this time when I make love to you. I want to watch every inch of your body flush with desire. I want to watch your face when you reach that perfect place. And I want to watch as you doze in perfect contentment when we've finished."

"But Matt—" Hanna could feel herself already start to blush at the very thought of him looking at her nude body in this bright light, although his words filled her with such desire she already thought she might explode.

Matt's lips quieted her protests, and soon she was lost to all thoughts except the hot rushing desire that his lips and hands were arousing in her.

They intermittently made love and dozed until afternoon dusk stole over the landscape outside. And each time they made love a scar from past hurts disappeared from Hanna's soul, until she felt complete and whole, as if she had never been that unhappy little girl who always felt as if she wasn't quite good enough to deserve her mother's or anyone else's love.

She came slowly awake from the contented sleep she had drifted into after their last round of lovemaking, to hear the shower running.

Feeling a sudden daring she had never felt before, she left the bed and went to the bathroom. She knocked timidly on the shower door, and asked, "May I join you?"

"I thought you'd never ask," laughed Matt, drawing her into the shower with him.

They soaped each other down, and wound up making love again while the water poured over their bodies.

"I just can't believe this is happening to me," Hanna said, throwing Matt a towel and using the one she had to dry her hair.

"Why can't you believe it? It had to happen sooner or later. A woman as sensual as you are had to eventually give in to someone and experience all you have to offer."

"I'm not talking about just anyone. I'm talking about you." The newly found bravado made Hanna want to share her long time infatuation with him.

"I—I used to fantasize about being a groupie for you when you were popular," she admitted, feeling her face flood with color.

"Really?" Matt's surprise seemed genuine.

"Want me to prove it?" Hanna asked.

"Woman, you're going to wear me down at this rate." Matt held onto the shower wall to demonstrate his weakness.

"No! I'm not talking about that! Come on."

Hanna led Matt to her room. After letting the towel she'd draped around herself slide to the floor, she slipped into a silk robe. Reaching into the closet, she pulled out all of the Matt Corbett collection she had saved all these years.

Matt's eyes grew larger as he watched the growing accumulation of cassettes, CDs, posters, several shirts with his picture on them, and a leather jacket just like the one he used to wear. He knew she had the life-size poster and he'd heard his songs playing the day he'd come into her room, but he had no idea she was this much of a fan.

Suddenly a thought struck Matt that rocked him back on his feet. Was this marriage just staged so the poor little rich girl could have one more thing she wanted? Did Will really just accidentally stumble upon him in a drunken stupor that night, or had they been stalking him?

He could feel the hair on the back of his neck prickle at the possibilities. But it was too late now to change things, especially since he was irrevocably in love with Hanna.

"I think my lo—infatuation for you is what kept me from getting involved with anyone all these years." She had almost said "love." How embarrassing that would have been! She mustn't let him know she was in love with him. She wanted him to feel free to walk away from her when the time came and he felt he needed to. She didn't want him to feel obligated to stay because he thought she loved him.

"I would fantasize about you picking me out of the audience and asking me to go with you on one of your tours, then you would fall in love with me—then I would remember that a man with your looks and talent would never be attracted to someone like me."

"So you arranged to marry me. That was the only way you thought you could have me, is that it?" Matt couldn't believe he had actually spoken his suspicions out loud.

"What?"

"Hanna, I'm sorry. I shouldn't have said that."

"What are you talking about? What did you mean?"

Realization dawned on Hanna as she looked at the stack of incriminating evidence lying around her. Matt thought she had been so obsessed with him she had arranged to marry him. It had been a horrible mistake to show him her collection.

Then anger flooded her. How dare Matt accuse her of trapping him into marriage!

"Excuse me? *I'm* not the one who misappropriated your funds. *I'm* not the one who got the IRS after your butt. And I'm sure as hell not the one who got you drunk and got you to sign those papers agreeing to marry me. In fact, I laughed Will out of the house when he told me you had agreed to marry me. And this damn marriage could have been avoided, anyway, if I'd only known then what I found out today. I would have let everything go to Grandfather's favorite charity like he threatened, and I would have just ridden off into the sunset and wouldn't have had to have worried about any of this crap."

"Hanna, please," Matt tried to calm her down.

"Just go, Matt. I need to clean this mess up. In fact, I'll just toss it in the dumpster! That way maybe you won't be worried about my obsession with you."

"No! Hanna, I was wrong to say what I said. I was wrong to even think it, but hell, being in the entertainment business screws up a person's mind. We have to start watching everything that goes on around us. Being suspicious of everyone and everything. You know what happened to me because I trusted my manager too much. I was wrong, but I won't let you shut me out. And this isn't junk. You've saved it all these years so it's special to you. You need to save it to show our children." Matt knew he had slipped up as soon as the words escaped his lips. But maybe Hanna was too angry to notice.

"Come on," he hurried, "tell me what you found out today."

But Hanna just stared at Matt. Had he really said "our children"? She was beginning to feel nauseated from the roller coaster of emotions she was on.

"Hanna, don't be angry with me. I really am sorry. Don't shut me out. Come on, baby, talk to me."

"Follow me," Hanna said, heading downstairs to get the papers she'd brought from the bank. Matt followed her, still wearing nothing but the towel he'd draped around himself when they left the bathroom.

Just as she reached for the manila envelope the phone rang, and she picked it up.

"Just a minute," she said into the receiver, then, looking puzzled, she handed the phone to Matt.

"Matt Corbett," he answered. "Molly? I thought I told you not to call on this phone!" Anger ripped through his voice. "I don't care! You're supposed to use my cell phone.

"Tonight?" He asked after a long pause. "Molly, I'm exhausted. Can't this wait until tomorrow?"

Finally, slamming the receiver down, Matt turned to Hanna. "I've got to—"

"I know, I know. You've got to go," she interrupted him. "Fine. This can wait. It wasn't important, anyway."

"Yes, it *is* important! But there's a problem at the stu—there's a problem that I have to take care of." He caught himself before he said "studio."

"I'll call you later," he promised as he dashed upstairs to dress.

"Sure," Hanna said under her breath, feeling sure she wouldn't hear from him tonight.

Picking up the envelope, she headed for her grandfather's office. She'd put the envelope in his safe until she needed to produce its contents.

What was she going to do about her mother and Will? Could she really turn them out into the cold, even knowing that neither of them was legally entitled to any of her inheritance? She really didn't think she could turn them away with nothing, but one thing was for sure, she would let them know she was aware of the circumstances. She would make sure Will knew he wasn't a Rockwell, and that anything he got was from the goodness of her heart. Oddly, that thought didn't make her feel any better.

Warm memories washed over her as she entered Grandfather's office. She hadn't been here since his death. It was almost as if he were sitting in the large leather chair behind the huge oak desk. His beloved books lined the bookshelves, and she felt tears swelling in her eyes, just knowing his hands would never again open and gently hold those books while his eyes pored over the words he loved so much.

"Oh, Grandfather," she sighed, sinking into the chair and burying her face in her folded arms, letting the tears flow.

Hanna didn't know how long she cried, but when her tears were spent, she leaned back in the chair and felt amazingly better. Almost as if she'd had a long talk with Grandfather. And somehow, she knew her life was going to be okay. That all would be well.

She stood and went to a book entitled *Keys to My Kingdom* and took it from the shelf. Just as Grandfather had shown her several years ago, the combination to the safe was written in code on the last page.

Taking the book, she went to a grouping of oil paintings on the wall and pushed one of the frames aside to expose a hidden safe. Soon she had the door open. She was about to insert the envelope when she saw another envelope in the back of the safe. Another surprise? Another secret? Or just another sweet memory from Grandfather?

With trembling hands, Hanna reached for the envelope and took out the contents. As she examined them closely, her pounding heart caused her ears to feel as if they would explode.

She was looking at a police report stating that her father's brakes might have been tampered with on the night of his death, and that her mother and Henri had been called in for questioning, but nothing had ever been proven.

Chapter 9

As if this information were too horrible for her to comprehend, Hanna crammed the contents back into the faded envelope and shoved it, along with her new information, back into the safe and quickly locked it as if afraid the information would escape into the universe for the world to see. She put the book back on the shelf and hurriedly left the office.

Back in the safety of her own room, Hanna sat and stared out the window. She understood why Grandfather could never tell her of his suspicions. He would never put that kind of thought into a child's mind if there weren't sufficient proof. And yet she was certain he'd left the information in the safe for her to find. Why did he want her to know? Did he really think her mother and Henri could do such a dastardly thing?

If Grandfather believed Henri could be in on murdering his only son, why would he have kept him in his employment all these years?

"Because he knew if he fired Henri, Mother would go with him, and he would lose me." The truth was as clear as crystal. "He loved me enough to endure the people he believed had killed his son," she mused aloud.

Suddenly, what her grandfather had given up for her, and the heritage he had left her, flooded in on Hanna and almost drowned her in an ocean of love and gratitude. And she was about to sell it all to a stranger. All of her memories. The home grandfather had worked so hard to have, and to keep.

Glancing at the clock, she realized it was too late to call the Realtor, but she would do it first thing in the morning.

She listened until the wee hours of the morning, but Matt didn't come home. When she finally fell asleep, she dreamed of Matt making love to someone named Molly.

The next morning, Hanna reached for the phone as soon as she awoke.

"I want to take my house off the market, today," she directed the voice that answered the phone at the real estate office.

"I'm sorry," the voice answered. "Everyone was in the office yesterday, and the papers were signed. Houston Couch signed by proxy for you. He said you'd directed him to sell the house. The new owner wants to take possession in two months. Houston said he'd let you know of the transactions."

"Why didn't you at least call me and make sure I hadn't had second thoughts?" Hanna glared at Houston Couch from across his desk. She had wasted no time in heading for his office as soon as she got off the phone with the real estate broker.

122

"Hanna, you told me to sell the house. You said I wasn't to argue with you. Remember?" Hanna couldn't understand the casual smile on Houston's face. He was usually more concerned about her feelings than he seemed to be today.

"Is there anything we can do to head the transactions off?" she asked. "Some kind of grace period or something?"

"No. I'm afraid not. I just wish you'd have listened to me when I tried to talk you out of putting your home on the market."

"Yeah, me too," Hanna agreed, resignedly turning to leave the office.

"Hanna," Houston's voice stopped her. "Things aren't always as they seem."

"What're you trying to say?" There was definitely a difference in Houston Couch today.

"Just keep that in mind for the next few weeks. You're going to be okay."

"Bye, Houston," Hanna said, shaking her head in bewilderment as she left his office.

As she pulled into the garage back at Rockwell Place, she saw Matt's motorcycle.

A sudden thrill shot through her, only to be replaced by a hollow space. She had to talk to Matt. She had to tell him the house was sold, and that they needed to make plans accordingly. She needed to ask him who Molly was, and if she was who he was spending his nights with.

Just inside the door of the house, she came to a sudden halt.

Roses filled the foyer and trailed into the living room. Rose petals covered the floor, making a carpet that led into the living room.

There she found Matt sitting on the couch. His head was at an angle, and she knew instantly that he had fallen asleep, waiting for her.

Love flooded her, shaking her to her toes. He had been waiting for her to come home. That, more than the roses, swept away all the hurt and anger she'd been feeling. She had never loved anyone like this before. How could she stay angry with him when she loved him so much? Still—there were some questions to be answered.

She leaned over to smell a single rose in a vase by itself.

"You like them?" His low, sleep-deepened voice was like a caress.

"They're beautiful," she answered, going to him and kneeling down in front of him.

He took her face between his hands and pulled her toward him. She came willingly and nestled between his legs. Her lips parted slightly to accept the gentle probing of his tongue. But before their desires overcame them, she pulled away and stood up.

"Matt, we have to talk." She sat in the chair opposite him.

"Don't you like roses?" Matt joked, not liking the seriousness in her voice.

"Please don't be flippant, Matt. We really need to talk."

"Okay. What do you want to talk about?"

"Do you think we'll be able to get through the conversation without a phone call from Molly?" Hanna couldn't believe she'd allowed that to slip out.

"Now who's being flippant?" Matt asked. "Hanna, Molly works in my friend Dave's office. I've been working on a project with Dave that's taking up a lot of time, and that's where I've been and that's why she called yesterday. I'm telling you the truth. Molly is a happily married mother of two. But thanks for being jealous," he added with a sudden twinkle in his eyes.

124

"Oh, you're so impossible," Hanna said, throwing a rose at him. She believed him because she wanted to, and suddenly felt her spirits rising a little. "Matt, the house has sold. We have to move out."

"When?"

"Two months, according to Houston."

"Then there's no real hurry," Matt concluded.

"Don't you know how fast two months can pass? We—I have to find a place to live. It's just so strange. No one's even come to look at the house. They don't even know what they're getting. This is the weirdest thing I've ever heard of."

"Well, if we don't find a place to live by the time the new owner wants to take possession, we could always go on that honeymoon we never got." Matt's voice was teasing, but Hanna's pulses leapt at the thought.

"Where would you want to go on a honeymoon?" she asked.

"Anywhere with you would be a honeymoon," he said, coming toward her.

"Yeah, that's a good, safe answer," Hanna said, dodging away from his outstretched hand. "Seriously. Where would you want to go?"

"I would love to go to that cabin of your grandfather's you talked about. That way we could be together with no interruptions. We could make love all night and sleep all day, or make love all day and sleep all night. Or—and this is better, we could make love all day and night and not sleep at all." Matt captured Hanna's wrist and pulled her against him

"Is that all you think about?" she asked, feeling her pulses leap at his touch.

"I told you, when you're around, it is. You make my blood run so hot, I might have a stroke if I ever did get a chance to be isolated with you."

Hanna watched his lips ascending to hers and forgot about tomorrow and all the troubles that lay ahead, as Matt lowered her to the bed of rose petals covering the floor. They made long, sweet love, then fell into an exhausted sleep with the wonderful scent of roses wafting around them.

Sometime later, Matt roused them enough to go upstairs to bed, where they both slept soundly for the first time in several nights.

Hanna awoke feeling rested and content. Matt was still asleep, so she eased from the bed and headed downstairs to get some coffee.

Sitting in her favorite chair on the deck, she looked out over the landscaped gardens. The peaceful scene with birds singing around her was one she had taken for granted, until now she knew it would no longer be hers.

Her grandfather's face appeared, unwanted, in her mind's eye. "Oh, Grandfather, what have I done?" Her heart ached with the loss she felt.

"Things aren't always what they seem. You're going to be okay." Houston Couch's face replaced Grandfather's.

What had Houston's words meant? And why had he looked so mischievous? Mischievousness was not one of Houston's more common attributes.

Did he know something else about the will that he hadn't told her yet? Frankly, she was getting tired of all the little ins and outs of Grandfather's will. Why did Grandfather have to make this such a mysterious affair? Why not just get it over with in one session and be done with it? She was sure he mistrusted her mother so much that he felt this was the only way to proceed. But what a pain!

"So here you are!" Matt's voice preceded him. He was trying to balance a cup of coffee and a Danish in one hand while he closed the sliding glass door with the other.

Hanna's pulses clamored at the sight of him. His only apparel was a pair of cut-off jeans and thong sandals. He hadn't bothered to put on a shirt, and the morning light glistened off the dark curls on his chest. Would she ever get tired of looking at him? Of being around him? Of making love with him?

He placed his coffee on the wrought iron table and slid a chair as close to Hanna's as it would go, then plopped down in it.

"What a beautiful, beautiful morning. Now, this is the way life should be. A good night's loving with a hot, steamy woman, then wake up and enjoy a morning like this with her. Life is good." He grinned at her before stuffing a big bite of Danish in his mouth.

Overcome by his antics, Hanna burst into a peal of laughter. He seemed rested and relaxed, and she loved him even more like this.

"Whatcha laughin' at, woman?" He asked around a mouthful of Danish. "You makin' fun of the way I eat?"

"Now would I make fun of you?" she asked innocently, between giggles.

"I just think you might be that kind of hussy, you hussy!" He crammed the last bite of pastry in his mouth, washed it down with coffee, and leaned toward her. "Gimmie a kiss, Baby."

"What is wrong with you?" Hanna squealed, slapping at him playfully.

"It just dawned on me this morning when I woke up that I'm truly happy for the first time in my life," Matt said, suddenly serious.

"You're the sexiest woman I've ever been with, and I love making love to you, but I also enjoy just being with you like this. I feel like a moonstruck kid this morning."

Hanna could only stare at Matt. Had he possibly just said those words, or was she dreaming? He hadn't said he loved her, but he had said all the other things that mattered. It was almost as good as hearing him actually say it.

She ached to tell him she loved him and felt the same way he had just described, but she was afraid to say too much. So she said nothing.

As they sat gazing deeply into each other's eyes, they were vaguely aware of a door slamming somewhere in the house. Then a voice pierced the air.

"Hanna! Where are you?"

"Mother?" Hanna said aloud, disbelief flooding her face.

"Well, damn!" Matt ground out through clenched teeth.

Chapter 10

"**There you are!**" her mother chirped as she came through the sliding glass doors, Henri and Will trailing closely behind her.

"The perfect little family," Matt muttered for Hanna's ears only.

"Why, Mother, what a surprise!" Hanna said, getting up from her chair to give her mother a token kiss of welcome. "I didn't expect you home from Europe so soon. And, Will, given the circumstances, I didn't expect you home for a long, long time." She could barely keep the sharpness from her voice when addressing her brother.

"Will told us you'd put the house on the market, and I came back as fast as I could to get this foolishness stopped!"

"It's too late, Mother, so you might as well go back to Europe and have some more fun." Hanna seemed to see her mother for the first time in her life. Mary Rockwell, or Mary Dupri as was actually the case, was a shallow, selfish woman.

As she stood beside the man who had helped her appreciate she was a worthwhile human being, Hanna realized all of her old intimidations and inhibitions were gone.

"What do you mean, 'it's too late?'" Will interjected.

"The house has already sold," Hanna said.

"Well, did you get the right price for it?" Mary asked hastily.

Matt spoke up. "She got the appraised price for the house."

Mary glared at him. "You just stay out of this. It's no affair of yours."

"Mother, Matt is my husband. What's my affair is his affair, and I would appreciate it if you didn't speak to him like that." Hanna couldn't believe she stood here defending Matt when a few weeks earlier it had been *him* defending her. But, vaguely, she wondered how Matt knew what the house had been appraised and sold for. "I'll tell you what, Mother. I'm sure you're all tired from your rushed trip back to the states, so why don't we meet at dinner tonight, and we can discuss what the future holds for us all."

"Oh, all right, dear, but I'm really anxious to know how the profit breaks down," her mother said, and turned and went back into the house with Will and Henri close on her heels.

"Does she mean what I think she means?" Matt asked.

"Oh, yes. She wants to find out how much her cut is going to be from the house."

"You're not really considering—?"

"Matt, would you like to come with me to Houston Couch's office?" Hanna interrupted him.

In less than an hour, Hanna and Matt were in the lawyer's office.

"Very interesting," Houston said, looking up from the papers Hanna had retrieved from the safe in Grandfather's office. "No, I wasn't aware of the investigation of Mary and Henri in regards to your father's death. But since nothing was proven, how you use this is strictly up to you. You'd probably even be able to reopen the case if you wanted to. I'm sure your grandfather didn't make a stink about it for the sake of adverse publicity."

"No, I don't want to reopen the case. But I'll use this information to get my point across to them tonight. Will you come to dinner with us? It'll be at seven o'clock."

"Sure, I'll enjoy seeing the look on everyone's faces when you drop your bombshell," he chuckled. "Seems kind of Sherlock Holmes-ish, doesn't it? Showdown at the dinner table! Your grandfather would be proud of you."

"Well, we'll see how it goes. But Houston, you said 'bombshell.' Make that plural—'bomb*shells*,'" Hanna said.
"What do you mean?" both men chimed together.

"You'll see," she said.

At seven o'clock, Hanna wasn't surprised to find everyone on time and seated around the huge formal table in the dining room. Cook had done a wonderful job of setting the table with just enough casualness to take some of the harshness away. Hanna glanced around the table at all the faces and wished she could read each one's mind.

Matt sat beside her, looking wonderful in a tan suit that enhanced his dark brown hair and piercing eyes. What was Matt's real game plan, she wondered? Even though she knew he was completely on her side tonight, and she knew no one would ever make her feel more like a woman than he did when they made love, and even though she knew she would love him forever, there were still too many unanswered questions surrounding him.

She watched her mother talking low and excitedly to Henri, whom Hanna had insisted join them for dinner, much to his surprise. Hanna realized as she watched her mother that she had never paid any attention when Mary talked to Henri. She was surprised at how Mary's face was alight with pleasure even after all these years of marriage to Henri. It was apparent that her mother really did love him. But she was too shallow to give up the money and social standing the Rockwell name could offer her, so she had lived a lie all these years.

For the first time in her life Hanna felt pity and compassion for her mother's weaknesses, and she realized the stronger *she* became, the more apparent her mother's weaknesses would become to her.

And Henri. Although at first he seemed extremely ill at ease sitting at the "big table," he soon relaxed and was now contentedly listening to whatever Mary was telling him. He was a handsome man, Hanna assessed. He, too, was dressed in a suit, and Hanna realized she had seen him out of his chauffeur's uniform only a few times in her life. Watching him closely, she was startled to see a sharp resemblance to Will. Why hadn't she noticed that before? It was so strange how one could overlook the obvious.

Had Will ever noticed it? Probably not. Will was so involved in his own little world he didn't notice much of anything, Hanna thought. As she switched her attention to her brother, she found him smirking at her.

"Well, Sis, you got everybody sized up in that calculating little head of yours?"

"You know, Will, it's the most amusing thing. I was just looking at everybody, thinking how little I know of each of you."

Suddenly, Mary and Henri stopped their conversation and looked at Hanna questioningly. But at that moment, Cook came in with the meal.

Conversation lagged while everyone began tasting the delicious food. Cook had really outdone himself tonight, and Hanna was glad. At least the food would be enjoyable, because what she had to say at the end of dinner, she was sure, certainly wasn't going to be enjoyed by most of them.

Hanna felt in total control tonight. It was the first time she had ever been in the same room with her mother and not felt like a second-rate citizen. Never again. She felt alive and excited. She was about to be free of everything that had held her back all these years. She was about to be her own woman, starting her life all over with no chains holding her back. No harsh words from her mother or Will could ever make her crawl back into her shell and hide. She felt like a bird that had been set free after a life spent in a cramped, little cage.

She looked up to find Houston, seated across the table from her, smiling as he watched the emotions play across her face.

"Hanna, you look exceptionally beautiful tonight," he said, tipping his wine glass to her.

"Well, thank you, Houston," she answered, tipping her glass in return, knowing he was taking great pleasure in what was about to come down.

Everyone was almost finished eating when Mary spoke up. "Hanna, this suspense is killing me. When are you going to tell Will and me how much money we have coming from the sale? We have to go back to Europe in a few days. As you know, it will be better for Will if he stays out of this country for a little while.

"And get this, Henri just found out his great uncle recently died and left him a huge old French castle and quite a large bank account, so we really do need to settle up here and get back there as soon as possible, so Henri can settle his business affairs."

No wonder her mother had looked so excited since she'd returned home. She was married to a wealthy man, and she thought she was going to get an additional chunk of money from the sale of Rockwell Place.

"Really, Henri? You're now a wealthy man with a home in France?" Hanna turned her attention to Henri, who was beginning to look uncomfortable with the whole subject.

"Yes," he answered, "I guess I'm one of those people who really did have a rich uncle." His embarrassed laugh gave credence to his discomfort.

"And did you know about all of this before you left for your European trip with Mother?" Hanna persisted.

"Well, uh, we—"

"No, Hanna," Mary interrupted, "he found out about his uncle after we were in France. The lawyers in charge of the estate had been trying to get in touch with him."

Hanna could tell when her mother was lying. The corners of her mouth started to twitch just the tiniest bit.

"So, Hanna, come on, how much?" Now Will was letting his eagerness show.

"How much what, Will?" Hanna was determined to hear him say it.

"How much money is coming to Mom and me from the sale of Rockwell Place?" He didn't seem embarrassed to ask the question. But why should he? He still believed he was a rightful heir.

"I'm afraid, Mother and Will, that you won't receive anything from the sale of Rockwell Place." Hanna's words dropped like an exploding bomb.

"*Whaaaat?*" Mary and Will screamed together.

"I'll sue your fat ass!" Will yelled, pointing at her, then looking quickly at Matt as if afraid Matt would come after him.

"Will! Shut up! I'll handle this," Mary screeched at Will, then turned on Hanna. "Surely you don't think you can get away with this!"

"And why wouldn't I be able to get away with it, Mother? Rockwell Place is mine, as I'm sure you know." Hanna couldn't believe how quiet and controlled her voice sounded, in comparison with her quaking insides.

"But, honey—" her mother suddenly changed tactics, whining—"you know how hard it's going to be for Will and me to live on just our allowance."

"Oh, yes, the allowance will be stopped at the end of this month, also," Hanna added to the brewing fury.

Matt and Houston watched as Hanna stood her ground and met the challenge from her mother and Will.

"That's it!" Will bellowed, slamming his chair back and starting to leave the room.

"Sit down, Will, there's more." Hanna's voice remained calm, but there was no mistaking the authority in her statement.

Surprised at Hanna's new demeanor, Will sank slowly back into his chair.

"Mother, were you ever going to tell me that you're married to Henri?"

"Oh, man, I can't take any more of this," Will said. "You have really lost your mind."

"Mother, tell him. For once in your life, be honest with your children," Hanna insisted.

She almost felt sorry for her mother as she watched the remaining color drain from her face.

"I don't know what you're talking about," Mary said, the corners of her mouth twitching more now.

Hanna reached down beside her chair and brought up a brown manila envelope. She took out the copy of the marriage license she had gotten from the bank lockbox.

"It says right here that you and Henri were married two weeks after my father was killed in that crash. Did you really think Grandfather was so stupid he didn't know what was going on between you and Henri?"

"Mary, it's over," Henri spoke up. "It's finally over. We can let the world know, now, how much we love each other. Stop denying it. We'll go back to France and start over. Make a new life for ourselves."

Hanna watched as her mother sank dejectedly into her chair, knowing she had lost the battle.

"So it's really true?" Disbelief sounded in Will's words. "But that shouldn't affect me, I'm still a Rockwell. Even if the old man never treated me as if I were, I should still get my allowance and a share of the house, since I won't even have a place to live now." He was almost crying from frustration.

Hanna looked from her mother to Will, seeing how pathetic and sad they both were, and wondered why on earth she had ever allowed them to bully her. But they were family and she had never, until now, wanted to break up that family, no matter how miserable it had been.

"Are you going to tell him, or am I?" Hanna continued, looking at her mother.

"Tell him what?" Mary asked, now acting as if in a fog, as if she couldn't quite comprehend all that was going on around her.

Hanna reached into the envelope and pulled out the copy of Will's birth certificate, with the blood test attached to it, and handed it to him.

"So that's it," Will almost whispered as he looked at Henri, then back at the paper in his hand. "That's why the old asshole treated me like he did."

"What?" Henri asked, reaching for the piece of paper in Will's trembling hand.

Henri read the birth certificate slowly, then glanced from Will to Mary as if he were in the twilight zone. "Why didn't you tell me, Mary?" Hurt sounded in his softly spoken question.

"I couldn't, Henri. I just couldn't." By now, Mary was softly crying into her cupped hands.

"Why? He's my son, and I missed his entire childhood. And you've allowed Will to grow up thinking he was fatherless, when his real father was here all along. Oh, Mary, did the Rockwell name really mean that much to you? If it did, why don't you just keep it, and not worry about openly becoming Mrs. Henri Dupri, like we talked about."

Horrified now that she would lose Henri and his inheritance, too, Mary slid her chair back and fell at Henri's feet. "Henri, can't you see? If old man Rockwell had thought for one moment that you knew about Will, he would have thrown us all out. You would have been without a job, and we would all have been homeless. I did it for us, Henri, please believe me."

Henri leaned down and gently raised Mary to her chair. Hanna was amazed at the love she saw in his eyes. "It really doesn't matter anymore, Mary. It's all behind us, and we can't change the past. We must just move on to the future."

Hanna glanced at Will, who sat as if frozen in place. She had never seen him this subdued. His life as he knew it had been a lie, and that had to come as a shock. And his mother, who had always been a strong support for him, had just crumbled in front of his eyes. His confusion must be complete.

Hanna almost decided against proceeding, but her mind was made up to clear all questions from the air tonight, so she spoke again.

"Mother, Henri, there's one other document that I want you to see and know that I'm aware of." She handed them the document indicating they'd been questioned regarding her father's death.

After reading what she handed them, they looked at her as if awaiting their doom.

"I'm not going to pursue reopening the case, and I truly don't want to know the answer, but I want you all to be out of this house by tomorrow night."

"Baby—" Her mother realized she was looking at a different Hanna than the little girl she had always been able to keep beaten down and subdued.

"Mother," Hanna interrupted her. "Someday, I want us to get to know each other as mother and daughter. And someday, I hope I'm able to forgive you for all the hurt you've caused me. But that day isn't here yet, so just go."

"But I have to tell you that Henri and I didn't tamper with your dad's car that night. I promise you I would never go that far. Your grandfather knew Henri and I had spent the afternoon together the night your dad had his wreck. He knew because he caught us together in the attic. He was so angry because your dad wouldn't throw me out that he went down to the police station and said just enough to the police to make them suspicious.

"They questioned Henri and me until we both thought we would scream, but they knew we didn't do it, so they didn't pursue the case. Please believe me, Hanna."

"That's the truth, Hanna," Henri spoke up. "Mr. Rockwell was justified in his anger, and I probably would have done the same thing he did, but we didn't try to hurt your dad. Three different mechanics agreed the brakes probably froze up on your dad that night, but even if the brakes had worked, they wouldn't have done any good on ice."

Watching Henri's and Mary's faces, Hanna believed they were telling the truth. She knew Grandfather was capable of causing anyone who crossed him a lot of problems, so it was easy to believe he might have deliberately led the authorities astray enough to put some scare into Mary and Henri. She breathed a deep sigh of relief that this much, at least, had been settled, but that didn't change the rest of the hurt they had caused.

"I hope that's the truth," Hanna said, suddenly weary from the mental turmoil of the night. Standing up, she shook Houston Couch's hand. "Houston, thank you for being here for me, as usual. I hate to be rude, but I think I'm going up to my room."

Matt had stood when she did, and now he walked beside her as she mounted the stairs.

"You were fantastic," he said in the low, assuring voice Hanna had grown to love.

"I was scared as hell," she admitted. "That is, until I realized for the first time how really cowardly and sad my mother is. Then I started to feel sorry for her. Matt, do you think I'll ever know how to love my mother?"

"Maybe in time you'll be able to have some kind of relationship with her. Maybe even become close to her. But do you really want to think about that right now?" He stopped her at the door to his room. "Or would you rather come on in here and let me relieve all that tension you have stored up inside?"

"Matt, would you just hold me for awhile? When I was a little girl, and I was hurt, Grandfather would hold me tight and I could feel the hurt go away. But it's been so long since I've had anyone to hold me."

Matt led Hanna to the bed, where he slowly undressed both of them and lowered them into the bed. He drew Hanna to him and held her while she let the tears flow quietly until a restful calm replaced the storm that had been brewing in her soul all night. He held her as she drifted into a peaceful sleep. And he continued to hold her throughout the night, knowing soon he must confess his love to her.

Yes, he must confess his love, but there were several other things he had to confess, as well.

Chapter 11

Matt's arm across her shoulders gave Hanna comfort as she watched her mother, Will, and Henri going down the driveway of Rockwell Place for the last time. Their good-byes had been strained and awkward, and Hanna felt a little sorry for them, knowing they were aware this would be the last time they would ever be in the home they had all grown so used to. She, too, would soon have to leave for the last time, and the thought brought fresh tears to her eyes.

Matt glanced at his watch. "Would you like to go with me to the Wildhorse Saloon in a couple of hours?" he asked. "I'm supposed to meet some friends down there at three o'clock."

"Sure," Hanna agreed, suddenly not wanting to be alone. "If you don't think your friends will mind if I tag along," she added as an afterthought.

"You're my wife, Hanna. If you aren't welcome with my friends, then they aren't my friends."

Acting on impulse, Hanna leaned into Matt and kissed the nape of his neck.

"What was that for?" he asked, taking her wrist and pulling her closer.

"For everything," Hanna answered, too overcome with emotion to go into detail.

She tried to pull away from him, but he held her wrist more tightly, and, lifting her hand to his lips, kissed her palm, sending a shockwave through her, melting her as it went. Then he moved his lips to the inside of her wrist and felt her throbbing pulse with his tongue before moving his mouth up to the bend of her arm, where he gently moved his tongue back and forth against the tender flesh.

Hanna could see her breasts rising and falling as her breathing became harder.

"You owe me for last night," he whispered, moving his mouth ever closer to her parted lips. "I was a good boy, and held you all night long, and it was the hardest thing I've ever done, to not make love to you."

He continued to whisper with his lips barely touching hers, driving her crazy with desire. "You are the most desirable woman I've ever met. No matter how hard I try, I can't keep my hands off you."

Now he was nibbling on her ear lobe as he talked. Each time Hanna turned her head to try to consummate the kiss he would elude her lips for some other part of her face, making her lips swell with wanting.

"Please, Matt," she begged, trying to capture his lips with hers.

"Is this what you want?" he taunted, snaking his tongue barely between her parted lips, only to take it back and kiss her closed eyes.

"Or is this what you want?" he asked, kissing each side of her mouth before tracing her bottom lip with his tongue.

"You're driving me crazy," she moaned, just before Matt claimed her lips in a hungry kiss that threatened to devour her.

Later in the car, headed for the Wildhorse Saloon, Matt glanced over at Hanna.

"You look perfect. You have that glow of someone who's just made love, and that light blue blouse makes your skin look like peaches and cream. You'll be perfect for tonight."

"What does that mean?" Hanna asked. "Perfect for tonight?"

"You'll see when we get there. These friends are special, and they're going to love you."

"Matt, you're making me nervous," Hanna scolded. "You've been acting strange all afternoon. What's going on?"

"Are you saying my lovemaking was strange?" he asked, trying to look hurt.

"No," Hanna chuckled, "that wasn't strange at all. In fact, it was quite wonderful," she admitted, before she realized what she was saying.

Matt leaned his head back and roared with laughter. "That's what I love about you. You forget not to be honest."

Hanna's heart lurched at his use of the word "love." She wished he wouldn't use the word so liberally if he didn't mean it. And she was sure he didn't mean it.

"Wait here and let me find my friends," Matt instructed Hanna, seating her at a table in the center of the room right in front of the nightclub's dance floor.

Stagehands were busy setting up equipment for some entertainer who apparently was going to perform a live show. Hanna hadn't been to the Wildhorse Saloon many times, but on a few occasions when she had been there, someone would perform live while people danced.

She looked around. She loved the life-sized sculptured horses placed about the room, especially the ones up in the balcony rearing up on their hind legs. People were gathered around some of the horses, getting their pictures made. Probably tourists, she mused.

A commotion to the side caught Hanna's attention. People were rolling in cameras as if they were going to tape the show for television or some other event. It must be a fairly big star if they were going to tape a TV special. Hanna's interest picked up. Who was it going to be? Probably a country music singer, but she couldn't imagine whom.

"Are you Hanna?" The voice came from a tall blonde who had walked up to the table.

"Yes."

"Matt asked me to keep you company," the blonde said, pulling out a chair. "I'm Molly."

So this was the woman who'd called and insisted on speaking with Matt. A long-legged, slim blonde. Hanna felt jealousy rear its ugly head.

"I'm Dave's assistant. I spoke with you once on the phone," she continued, as if sensing Hanna's discomfort.

"Yes, I remember." Hanna tried to act nonchalant. "Matt said you had children." She wasn't trying to be devious; she just needed a little assurance.

"Yes, Mike is five, and Della is two. They're wonderful kids, but such pains in the ass sometimes." Molly wrinkled her nose to make her point more believable.

Hanna laughed out loud, suddenly feeling all was right with the world. Molly didn't seem at all like the kind of woman who would fool around with a married man, no matter what his circumstances were.

"Well, it looks like you two have hit it off." Matt's voice was close as he leaned over and pulled a chair beside Hanna's. "Hanna, this is Dave." He introduced a short, stocky man with a receding hairline who had the most alive, twinkling blue eyes Hanna had ever seen. She immediately liked him.

"Hello, Hanna," Dave said, taking her hand and kissing it. "Matt's been telling me what a wonderful woman he married. But I think, as a friend, I should have gotten to meet you a long time ago." He sounded wounded.

"I totally agree," Hanna said, enjoying the friendly banter.

Just then an emcee went to the microphone and started testing for volume and clarity.

"Hanna, I have to go, now," Matt said, kissing her quickly on the cheek and winking at Dave and Molly, who stayed seated. He was gone before Hanna could question where he was off to.

A large crowd had gathered in the saloon, and there was beginning to be standing room only, which added to Hanna's suspicions that a big star was going to be there tonight. She felt a ripple of excitement run through her. She had always loved live performances.

The emcee started talking again. "Ladies and gentlemen, and all you rednecks—" this brought a huge roar of applause from the audience—"I am elated to be the one to announce our performer

145

tonight. In fact, we're taping the vocal part of his new video, which will be out soon, to debut the new single off of his latest—well actually, his *first*—country album. But this guy isn't new to some of us. Some of us knew and loved him back when he was one of them outlaw rock stars. Y'all put your hands together for Matt Corbett, singing, *Lady, Love of My Life!*"

The crowd broke into a roar of applause, and the ones sitting rose to a standing ovation as Matt bounded onto the stage. After he had left Hanna he'd slipped into his trademark black leather jacket.

Hanna was too stunned to stand. Suddenly she was a teenager again, watching Matt on stage in the same black jeans and leather jacket. Her heart pounded as he started singing a steamy love song she had never heard before.

As he sang, he made his way toward her. She wasn't aware of the cameras and lights that followed him, or even of the bright spotlight that settled on her. She wasn't aware of the love light that shined in her eyes as she watched him approach her. She was only aware that Matt Corbett was kneeling in front of her and singing into her eyes. She was living her wildest teenage fantasy.

The song's lyrics were about a man who was so in love with a woman that every thought he had was centered around her.

The pounding of Hanna's heart in her ears almost drowned out the music, and she wondered if she was going to faint. But she heard the words of the song and almost felt as if Matt were really singing them to her, personally. *If only that were the case*, she thought wistfully, as she reached up on impulse and laid her palm gently against his cheek.

As if on cue, the song ended, and Matt took her hand and pressed his lips into her palm before standing.

"Ladies and Gentlemen," he announced into the mike, "this is my beautiful wife, for whom I wrote this song."

As Hanna sat in mesmerized silence watching Matt perform several more newly written songs that were to be on his new album, she realized he had his career back on track. Or, more appropriately, he was about to launch a new career. From the way the audience was reacting to his songs, he would be a great success in the country music field. It was obvious they loved him.

What now? Hanna was sure Matt would go on tour to promote his new career and album. Where would that leave her?

Totally alone. He wouldn't need her anymore. The thought came quietly, unbidden, unwanted, into her mind. As complete loneliness settled over her, Hanna became aware that the crowd was yelling at Matt to do some of his older rock songs.

"Okay, okay," Matt's deep voice spoke into the microphone, captivating his audience. "I found out after I got married that my wife was a devoted fan of my past career, so I'm dedicating this song to her." And he proceeded to sing Hanna's favorite song.

Hanna watched in rapt attention, never taking her eyes off of his, as he sang. She wasn't aware of how many times the camera lingered on her face, capturing her look of love and enchantment. She was only aware of Matt Corbett, her teenage idol, singing to her from on stage.

When the show was over, Matt informed the audience that he would hang around for a while to sign autographs and make pictures with anyone who was interested, and to Hanna's amazement almost every person in the place lined up to talk with him, get his autograph, and have their picture made with him.

Expecting the night to go on forever, Hanna resigned herself to sit and wait for the fans to clear out. So she was surprised to look around and find Matt standing beside her.

"Were you impressed?" he asked, almost like a little boy waiting for approval for a job well done.

"Oh, Matt." Words failed Hanna. "You were—you are—I'm so proud of you!" She ended her stuttering by throwing her arms around his neck.

"Now, that's the kind of reaction I was hoping for!" Matt laughed, holding Hanna tightly before pulling away from her and saying, "Listen, why don't you take the car and go on home? Dave can bring me when this is all over. He'll have to stay here with me anyway. You'll be bored to tears if you hang around."

Not relishing the thought of watching the fans swoon over Matt, especially the female ones, Hanna agreed that it would be best for her to go home. She and Molly walked together to the parking garage to find their cars.

"Hanna," Molly hesitantly opened the conversation. "Are you going with him when he leaves on the tour next week?"

"Next week?" Hanna was devastated to find out Matt would be leaving so soon.

"Oh, no! You didn't know, and I've opened my big mouth! Matt's going to kill me!" Molly was almost in tears.

"It's okay," Hanna tried to soothe her. "I'm sure Matt will tell me tomorrow. But I don't know if I can go that soon or not. I have to finalize the selling of Rockwell Place before I can leave town."

"So he hasn't told you about that yet, either?" Molly's eyes were wide with concern.

"About what?" Hanna asked, curiosity edging her voice.

"Hanna, please don't tell Matt I mentioned the house. He'll really be pissed at me. Please?" Molly seemed overly concerned about Matt's reaction.

"Okay, but tell me what you're talking about," Hanna pleaded.

"Hanna, I can't. I really have to go." Molly ran toward her parked car, leaving Hanna standing alone and baffled.

Hanna's head ached as she climbed into bed. A thousand questions had flitted across her weary brain since she'd left Molly.

On the one hand, she was so proud for Matt. He seemed to have gotten his life back on track, and she knew that must mean a lot to him. But on the other hand, she knew that his gain was surely her loss. He would leave her now, and never look back.

But why hadn't he told her what he was doing? All those nights she thought he might be with another woman, he was obviously working on his album. Why hadn't he let her share in the joy of the pursuit of his dream?

Because he only needed you for the money, a little voice in her head whispered.

No, that's not true, Hanna argued with the voice. What about the wonderful way he had made love to her, and all those beautiful words he had whispered?

Some men will do whatever they have to do to get sex, the little voice persisted. And this time Hanna didn't argue, because she was afraid the little voice was right.

She drifted into a restless sleep, dreaming of being chased by fans who were trying to keep her away from Matt when she really needed to talk to him to tell him something important.

Hanna turned and tossed for several hours before finally giving up and getting out of bed. No use to keep lying there if she couldn't sleep.

Slowly the dreams of the night drifted back to her, dimly at first, then becoming clearer as she tried to decipher each one. But one dream kept eluding her consciousness. Something about being chased by fans who wouldn't let her tell Matt something. But what was she trying so hard to tell him? Somehow, now that she was awake, it seemed very important to know what she was trying to tell him.

Out the window, the sun was coloring the eastern sky a beautiful red hue. Passing Matt's room on her way downstairs, she saw his bed was still made, and hadn't been slept in.

What had he done all night? And with whom? Now she wished she'd insisted on staying with him until every autograph had been signed and every picture had been taken.

Sitting at the huge oak table alone, looking up into the watchful eyes of Grandfather's portrait, a tranquility settled over Hanna like none she had ever known. It was almost as if Grandfather was there with her, smiling calmly at her as he always did, and reminding her that life was hers to live as she chose.

Grandfather had always been there to encourage her when her self-esteem was down around her ankles, which is where it always seemed to stay in those days. He would get so frustrated at her sometimes because she let the things her mother and Will said affect her so much.

Why was it so easy to believe the negative things they said to her? And why was it so hard to believe the positive, uplifting things Grandfather said to her?

Because she chose to believe the negative things.

There it was. Just as Grandfather had been trying to tell her all those years. How she lived her life was her choice. What she believed about herself was her choice. And that was what Matt had been trying to make her realize, too.

Well, she had come a long way, baby. She hoped Grandfather knew how much she had changed in the last few months. Never again would she allow another person to determine the way she felt about herself.

And it wasn't just because Matt had made slow, maddening love to her and told her all the things a woman needs to hear. Even when Matt was no longer in her life, she knew she would still hold onto this new self-image she now had. She knew she was worth loving, even if Matt didn't love her. And she knew she was worth loving, even if she never found a man who loved her.

Suddenly the elusive dream interrupted her thoughts. This time she remembered what she had been trying to tell Matt.

She needed to tell him she was pregnant.

Chapter 12

Pregnant?

Hanna jumped from her chair and bolted up the stairs to her bedroom to check the calendar she kept hanging on the wall.

Two weeks late! "Oh, please, God, please don't let this be happening," she prayed, sinking to a sitting position on the side of the bed, clutching her head in both hands.

But deep down inside, she knew it was true. Her periods were never late. Now she understood the slight queasiness she felt the last few mornings when she had first gotten out of bed. She'd noticed it, but just assumed it was because she wasn't getting much rest at night.

She was pregnant with Matt Corbett's baby. She couldn't tell Matt until she knew for sure, but how would he react? Especially now, when he was just getting his career back on track. Would a baby make a difference in whether he stayed with her or not?

She couldn't tell him. Not yet. Not until she knew if he planned to leave her, now that they didn't need each other anymore. If he chose to leave, then she'd tell him about the baby after the divorce. That way he wouldn't feel obligated to stay with her if he didn't love her.

When was she going to find out who bought Rockwell Place? She'd never heard of anything as strange as this situation. She'd sold her house and, according to her last bank statement, the down payment had been deposited into her account by Houston Couch, and she had never seen or even talked to the new owners.

Hanna reached for the phone.

"Houston? I need some answers about the buyers of Rockwell Place. You said they wanted to move in in two months, but does that mean I have a solid two months before I have to move out? Or do they want me out sooner than that so they can actually be in the house in two months?"

"Actually, I don't think the new owner would mind if you stayed there indefinitely." Houston sounded vague. "There doesn't seem to be any hurry for you to move. Two months was just a time we came up with at the time of the sale."

"No hurry for me to move? Who buys a house and then doesn't want to move into it? Houston, tell me what is going on! Something is wrong with this situation, and I believe you know what it is, so tell me!"

"Now, calm down, Hanna," Hanna had never realized how patronizing Houston's voice could be at times when he didn't want someone challenging his word.

"No, I won't calm down, Houston. I'll call someone who'll tell me what I need to know. I have the right to know who bought my home. I'm not a child anymore, Houston. I grew up while you weren't looking." She hung up the phone as she heard him attempting to say something.

"Hanna, where are you?" Matt's voice preceded him up the stairs.

Hanna, in the act of dialing the real estate office, lowered the receiver back to the base. "In here, Matt," she answered, feeling her pulse leap at the sound of his voice.

He stopped at the barely cracked door and asked, "Can I come in?"

"Yes," Hanna answered, not getting up from the side of the bed, where she had been sitting to use the phone.

Matt had a look about him that Hanna had never seen. He fairly beamed with happiness.

"I did it, baby. I got my life back," he said, plopping down on the bed beside her. "What do you think about last night? About me getting my career back? Are you happy for me—for us?"

No reasons as to why he was gone all night. No apologies. Not even a welcoming kiss.

The old Hanna would have broken into tears from the hurt she felt, but the new Hanna felt a sudden surge of anger.

"Boy, you have the balls, don't you! You think you can just waltz in here as if nothing was wrong, with a big stupid grin on your face, and I'm supposed to melt at your feet! Where the hell were you last night? Do you think I'm supposed to believe you signed autographs all night? Is it just impossible for you to pick up a phone and let me know you won't be home? I forgave you twice before, but this is getting old."

"Baby, wait—" Matt tried to reach for Hanna's hand, but she pulled away from him and started pacing the floor.

"'Baby, wait,' my ass! Baby waited all night, and you didn't show up! Baby's tired of waiting. I'm tired of waiting to find out who bought my home. I'm tired of waiting to find out when I have to move, and I'm tired of spending nights waiting to see if you're coming home or not. Well, I'm not waiting anymore. I'm calling to find out who owns Rockwell Place. I'm going to find out when I need to be out of here. And you can bet I won't spend another restless night waiting for you to show up!"

By now, Hanna was out of breath from the tirade she had let loose with, and Matt was staring at her with his mouth open.

"Damn! I didn't think you had a fit like that in you!" Matt said, reaching for the phone. "I'm impressed. Hello, Dave? I've got you on Hanna's speakerphone. Will you tell her where I was all night, please?"

Hanna expected anything but the loud roar of laughter from the other end of the line. "Matt, you in the doghouse, old boy?" Dave choked out.

"When you get finished enjoying yourself, just tell her where we were," Matt said with a grin on his face.

"Okay, Hanna, this is the truth. When it came time for the Wildhorse to close, there were still scadoodles of fans waiting to get Matt's autograph, so we told them to follow us over to the studio, and they did, and we just a little while ago got finished with them. This is a very good sign that Matt's fans are back with him even though he's changing from rock to country. Hanna, the big boys are saying Matt may be the next Garth Brooks! I'm telling you, lady, you're married to one of country music's next big stars. Can I go now? I really need some sleep."

"Can he go now?" Matt asked Hanna with raised eyebrows.

"Bye, Dave. You better not be lying for him." Hanna hung up the receiver. "I'm sorry," she said, as Matt came toward her.

"I think I like you being jealous of me," Matt said, taking her hands in his.

"Jealous?" Hanna laughed. "In your dreams!" But suddenly, she became serious. "Matt, I really am proud of you. I almost passed out last night when you bounded up on that stage and started singing."

"Did you like the song?" Matt's eyes held hers, waiting for her answer.

"I love all of them. They're really great. I didn't know you could write like that." Hanna deliberately avoided the question about the song Matt supposedly wrote for her.

"But did you like the one I wrote for you?" Matt persisted.

"Did you really write it for me?" Hanna couldn't believe Matt Corbett had actually written a song for her.

"Do you remember the day you stopped by my door and were listening to a song on my tape recorder, and I kind of got snippy with you?"

"Yes," she answered.

"I was in the process of writing the song then, but I didn't want you to hear it until it was finished. Yes, the song is for and about you, Hanna."

Hanna was about to ask him to sing it to her again when his cell phone rang.

"Yes?" Matt inquired. After listening for a few moments, a smile spread across his face. "Yeah, I know what you mean, Houston, she's been raising hell with me this morning, too." He winked at Hanna as he talked.

Why was Houston Couch calling Matt on his cell phone, talking about her? Hanna wondered. This seemed highly unusual.

"Yes, we finished it three days ago. I sure wish you could have been at the Wildhorse last night. We really had a good turnout."

So Houston knew about Matt's budding country music career? Maybe Matt was using Houston as his lawyer now. That made more sense.

"Okay. I'll tell her. Look, you have my will, if she kills me, okay?"

Hanna could tell Matt and Houston were having a good laugh at her expense. She just couldn't understand why.

Finally, Matt ended the phone call.

"Can we go down and get some coffee? We really need to have a long conversation, but since I've been up for over twenty-four hours, and some of the adrenaline is wearing off, I'd better tank up on some java to keep me going."

Sitting at the table, Hanna waited impatiently for Matt to tell her what the phone call from Houston was about.

"Hanna, before I tell you what Houston and I were discussing, I need to ask you something. I know that our marriage started out as just a convenience for both of us. You needed me, and I needed you.

"I didn't tell you what I was trying to accomplish with my music, because I didn't want you to know if I failed. I know that sounds silly to you, but I felt like a loser anyway, and I hated that you thought I just married you for your money. I wanted to make my own way, so I could be worthy of your love. So I could declare my love to you as a man standing on his own."

"Your love?" Hanna wondered if her ears were deceiving her.

"Yes. My love. I love you, Hanna. I want to spend my life with you. Would you like to be my one and only groupie? Please say yes."

Hanna could only stare into Matt's earnest eyes. Could this be possible? Was Matt Corbett really declaring his love for her? Her head was spinning, and she was afraid she was really going to pass out this time. Her fantasy was actually coming true.

"Hanna?" Matt slid to the floor in front of her and slipped his arms around her waist.

Hanna placed her hands on each side of his face and lifted it to hers.

"Oh, Matt! You've just made me the happiest groupie in the world," she whispered. "Yes, I want to spend my life with you. Whether it's on the road, or anywhere else. I love you, Matt. I think I always have, and I know I always will."

She lowered her lips to his in a kiss that sealed their love.

"Wait, there's something else I need to tell you," Matt said, sitting back in his chair. "Houston called saying you were determined to know who bought Rockwell Place?"

"Yes, I think it's time I knew."

"Lucy Holmes bought Rockwell Place." At Hanna's blank expression, Matt continued. "My aunt, Lucy Holmes. She's the one you heard me talking about getting money from, on the phone that day with Dave. You thought I was talking about you.

"But I convinced my Aunt Lucy to put up the money to jump start my career. It's called a "backer." She also put the money down and acted as my purchaser, since I didn't want you to know I was the one buying Rockwell Place."

"What? You bought Rockwell Place? But why?" Hanna didn't know how many more surprises she could stand in one day.

"Because Houston said you were determined to put it on the market, and I was afraid you would regret it one day, so I bought it back for you. Besides that, I kind of wanted our children to grow up at Rockwell Place. I've grown to love this old house."

Finally, Hanna found her voice. "Speaking of children, Matt—"

Epilogue

A contented smile played on Hanna's lips as she sat and watched her mother play with Matthew Rockwell Corbett. "Little Rockie," as Matt fondly called their two-year-old son.

Matthew was a clone of his father, except for Hanna's green eyes. He also seemed to have his father's fatal charm. She pitied all the little girls who were destined to fall victim to the young Matthew Corbett. With his black hair, green eyes, and lethal charm, she knew many hearts would break before he found the right love of his life.

Life had changed dramatically for Hanna in the two years and nine months of her marriage. Matt had, indeed, become a huge country music star. But his career had taken off in Europe equally as successfully as it had in the States. He had insisted that she and Matthew travel with him because he didn't want to be separated from them a single minute longer than it took to stand on stage and deliver his show. As soon as he could exit the stage he'd be back on their private bus.

They had decided on a bus rather than trying to keep Matthew confined to hotel rooms when they were on tour, which was most of the time. They had purchased the largest touring bus they could get. Matthew had plenty of room to romp, and even a designated play area. They wanted it to seem as much like a real home to him as possible. They had a driver who delivered the bus to wherever Matt would be performing, and Matt, Hanna, and Matthew would fly there on their private jet, then stay in the bus for as long as Matt performed in the area.

Except when they were in Europe, as they were now. When Matt performed in Europe, Hanna and Matthew stayed with Henri and Mary.

Hanna still couldn't believe the change in her mother. After Mary realized that her connection with the Rockwell name and fortune was severed, she happily became Mrs. Henri Dupri. And in so doing, her whole personality changed, almost like a butterfly metamorphosing from a caterpillar.

She'd become the loving mother that Hanna had always dreamed of, and she absolutely doted on little Matthew. She was a model grandmother, and Hanna caught glimpses of the mother she had been cheated out of all her life. But catching those glimpses enabled Hanna to go through healing periods that helped her understand and forgive her mother.

Mary had apologized repeatedly to Hanna for being such a horrid mother, and Hanna had just as repeatedly forgiven her and assured her that everything was wonderful now.

And everything *was* wonderful now. She was surrounded by a loving family. She wished somehow that Grandfather could know how it had all turned out. She wished he could know how happy her life had become and how much she loved him and appreciated the sacrifices he'd made in his life to try to secure her future joy.

"Happy, Sis?" Will whispered, as he leaned over and placed a kiss on Hanna's cheek.

"Very," she answered, as she reached up and patted his face.

Will was the other surprise. He had met a woman five years older than him who seemed to be exactly what he needed. They had gotten married six months after they met, and had been blissfully happy ever since.

Judith, a French designer, loved Will with all her heart, but she had let him know up front that she wouldn't put up with any of his former attitudes, and as a result, he had accepted a position in her already established business, and together they were in the process of becoming very successful. He'd proven to be extremely business-minded, and was surprising them all with his ability to negotiate and follow through with the deals that were needed for the growth of their company.

He had also apologized to Hanna for the horrid way he had always treated her, and they were learning how to relate to each other as siblings.

Matt would be home tonight, and tomorrow they would leave to go back to Rockwell Place for a rare two-month stay. Matt would be back in the studio cutting his third album, which the "powers that be" predicted would be his biggest yet.

Hanna loved those brief chances to go home to Rockwell Place. She shuddered each time she thought about how close she had come to losing it. Little Matthew loved "his home," as he called it, and got excited each time they were able to go there for a while. Hanna knew that eventually they would have to make a decision as to whether she stayed at Rockwell Place and put Matthew in school, or if they would hire a tutor to travel with them, but that was a long time away, and she didn't have to worry about that yet.

"Catch, Uncle Will," Matthew yelled, throwing a rubber ball before Will was expecting it, and hitting him on the side of his head.

"Honey, be careful," Hanna admonished.

"He's doing just fine," Judith said, laughing at Will rolling around on the floor as if he had been mortally wounded. "He needs to be hit upside the head more often."

"I'll show you what I need, woman," Will said, lunging for her as she squealed and dodged his advances.

They were all enjoying a good laugh when Matt's voice interrupted them. "Sounds like you started the party without me," he teased, coming through the door.

"Daddy!" Matthew yelled, and bounded for Matt.

Hanna watched as Matt gathered their son up in his arms for a big hug. She would never lose the thrill of seeing Matt come through the door. Her love for him grew each day. He was a wonderful father, but an even better husband. Their lovemaking seemed to get better each time, and she wondered how anyone could talk about a marriage losing its spark.

Matt's eyes caught and held Hanna's. The familiar charge of electricity shot through her as he came to her and gave her a kiss, still holding Matthew in his arms. For a moment, the three of them stood with their arms around each other.

"This is going to be hard to do when we have a house full of kids," Matt teased.

Hanna gently placed a hand on her stomach. She had some surprising news for Matt as soon as they got home to Rockwell Place.

About the Author

Pat Ballard lives in Nashville, TN. She writes motivational romance novels with Big Beautiful Heroines to show that plus-size women can be just as sexy, romantic, and exciting as their slim sisters.

Visit Pat at www.patballard.com.

Check out other books by Pat — and more — **at the Pearlsong Press website at www.pearlsong.com.**

www.ingramcontent.com/pod-product-compliance
Lightning Source LLC
Chambersburg PA
CBHW052135170626
46812CB00004B/1431